KJELL WESTÖ was born in 1961 in Finland. Since his literary debut in 1986 he has published three collections of poetry, two books of short stories and three novels. He is one of the leading Swedish-language authors in Finland today.

EBBA SEGERBERG teaches English at Washington University in St Louis, Missouri. She is the translator into English of several crime novels by Henning Mankell.

Kjell Westö

LANG

Translated from the Swedish by
Ebba Segerberg

CARROLL & GRAF PUBLISHERS
NEW YORK

LANG

Carroll & Graf Publishers
An Imprint of Avalon Publishing Group Inc.
245 West 17th Street
11th Floor
New York, NY 10011

AVALON
publishing group incorporated

First Carroll & Graf edition 2006

Library of Congress Cataloging-in-Publication Data is available.

ISBN-10: 0-7867-1724-6
ISBN-13: 978-0-78671-724-8

9 8 7 6 5 4 3 2 1

Printed in the United States of America
Distributed by Publishers Group West

LANG

I

One night in November, almost three years ago now, the phone rang. My wife, Gabriella, who is a lighter sleeper than I am, woke up and started to shake me violently. Like my friend and colleague Lang, I have always been at ease with the sudden twists and turns of city life. But Gabi is still marked by her rural upbringing. She is both determined and robust, but has a tendency to be rattled by the unexpected. That autumn had already brought its share of worries; Gabi's son Mattias, whom she had when she was only nineteen, had moved to Åbo to study at the university. And then Gabi's father had a heart attack. So when Gabi woke me up that night she was beside herself.

"Someone's died!" she managed to say. "Wake up, Konni! Dad or Matti is dead, I know it. This is just that kind of night."

Reluctantly I opened my eyes and found myself in a real-life *film noir*: the wind wailing on the rooftop, sheets of rain pouring down the bedroom window, the door half open to the hall and living room, the monotone rings of the phone echoing through the apartment, a car motor growling outside, the headlights of a night bus making their way up the living room wall as it drove up Topeliusgatan before turning down the narrow shaft of Runebergsgatan.

"Why don't you answer it since you're already up?" I said

sourly, but to no avail since Gabi stayed frozen in terror, the blankets wrapped around her and only her feet sticking out. The phone kept on ringing. I walked stiffly into the hall and made my voice as gruff as I could. It was Lang. He sounded strained, not his usual ironic drawl. Lang said he was in a hell of a spot, he used just those words: "a hell of a spot".

"A living nightmare," he said.

I didn't take him terribly seriously. I was used to Lang making these kinds of calls from time to time, always after midnight and after at least a couple of drinks, always on minor even banal pretexts. So I asked him if he knew what time it was, told him that he had frightened Gabi half to death, that she thought her dad must have up and died. Then I added, pretty childishly, that if Lang had run out of condoms he had called the wrong place. This was a reaction to the kind of lifestyle Lang had acquired in the past few years since his divorce, a life I often envied. But Lang ignored my sarcastic remarks and his voice only took on a more desperate intensity.

"It's nothing like that," he said. "I need help. Something terrible has happened and I need someone level-headed to talk to. Do you have a shovel? A sturdy one, not the kind with the plastic handle that breaks in the middle if you put your whole weight on it."

Lang and I go back a long way, and I've never been very good at saying no to him. He's the opinionated and charismatic type, hard to overrule. Gabi thinks I'm too much of a push-over, that I let Lang and certain other childhood friends use me, and she may have a point. Fifteen minutes later I was dressed, had been up to the attic and was waiting on Tölö Square with a sturdy steel shovel in my hand. I was already having second thoughts. The rain was pouring down and the square was deserted, but there were still people at the Tin Tin Tango and in Mama Rosa's Bar, and the customers seated next to the window were regarding me and my shovel with bemused interest. Lang had told me he would come there in his car and this served only to increase my anxiety. Lang was a night owl, but he rarely drove after midnight: he drank too much for that. When at last he drove up at high speed he wanted immediately to head out of town. He was astonishingly pale, his teeth clenched, and his hands squeezed the steering wheel of the Celica so tightly that his knuckles really did go white. His sudden appearance on the scene in the square had only fanned the idle curiosity of the spectators and that was when I grew definitively fearful. My intuition started whispering to me in that certain way: Alert! Suspicious behaviour! Danger!

So I explained to Lang, as casually as I could manage, that he couldn't drive me out to the spiritual darkness of suburban Esbo or rural Sibbo or whatever he was planning until he had told me what was going on. My rudely awakened stomach started to grumble and I suggested that we get a beer and a hamburger at a night café while he said what he had to say – my treat. Lang agreed to that and we drove along the wet and slick – several times I asked him to slow down – Mannerheimvägen to a petrol station café at Brunakärr. There I discovered that Lang was in such a state of shock and confusion that he couldn't keep his end of the bargain. He started his story way back in the past, telling it without regard either for chronology or logic. It was as if he supposed that these random and disordered anecdotes would give me a sense of how his eyes had slowly opened to the reality of where his love for Sarita was going to lead him. Sarita, Marko and Miro's names all came up again and again and when Lang's tense account began to approach the present I already knew that something appalling had happened, and I even suspected what. My suspicions were confirmed in part by the raw red marks on Lang's neck which he tried to conceal by keeping his coat collar up. In part, too, they were fuelled by the many police dramas and other thrillers on television that had given any male of my sort of age and background certain intuitions with regard to criminal activity: that, at any rate, is my only explanation for the quickness of my thinking that night.

Thus I didn't wait for Lang to finish: I put to him a brutally frank question as to why he was driving out of Helsinki in the middle of the night. Lang confessed without any more beating around the bush and I at once told him that my involvement in the matter ended right then and there, at the Teboil café in Brunakärr at 2:50 a.m., the night of November 15, 2000. I made plain to him that regardless of whether it had come about out of love or hate, he had to face the consequences on his own for what he had done. Our friendship was of more than thirty years standing and had been through a lot, but not even that was grounds for sharing with him the kind of front page headlines I could see coming.

"It's not fair to ask something like this of a friend," I said, advising him to drive straight to the police station in Böle and give himself up. Lang shook his head and started to cry. We sat there a little while longer, whispering at each other across the table. The night was black and wet and I gave in: against every instinct, I lent him my shovel.

I was nervous about that whole business with the shovel throughout the duration of the trial and for as long as the story regularly featured in the papers. The evening tabloids ran screaming headlines and Police-TV asked the public repeatedly for witnesses who could shed light on Lang's activities that night. It's not hard to imagine how tarnished the image of the presently well-behaved body of Finnish writers would have become had it transpired that not one but two of their number were involved.

But Lang was loyal, he never revealed the identity of the

shovel's owner, always maintaining it was his own. For some reason not one of the customers of the Tin Tin Tango or of Mama Rosa's stepped forward to describe the man who Lang had picked up on Tölö Square that night. Some witnesses had come forward about an unidentified man whom Lang had been engaged in conversation with at a petrol station café in Brunakärr (they had me down as bald, which is ridiculous since having a high hairline is scarcely the same thing as being bald). Lang emphatically denied that such a meeting had taken place. He admitted that he had shared a table with a man in his forties, but said that he had been a complete stranger and at most they had exchanged a few remarks about the foul autumn weather, and the tribulations of insomnia.

I've been jealous of Christian Lang as long as I can remember. He had a steady girlfriend by the time he was thirteen, and hair on his chest by sixteen. He was captain of the ice hockey and the soccer teams and graduated from high school with five *laudaturs* and exam marks averaging well above nine out of ten. By the age of twenty-five he had received half a dozen prizes for his first novel and ten years and a handful of novels and a collection of essays later he had transformed himself into a talk show host, a literary showman whose charisma was larger than life and who lured his guests into animated and deliciously personal conversations.

This time his place in the spotlight was nothing to envy. One reason I managed to escape was through my very anonymity, my unremarkable appearance. In a way, I had my lacklustre career to thank for my continued freedom. The only one who knew the truth was Gabi. During the torment of those weeks of the trial she looked at me in the way that only a wife can look at a husband whose shovel was used on a black November night to bury a dead body.

II

Lang never dreamed his relationship with Sarita would last so long. That was what he repeatedly told me in long conversations and letters after he had decided that he was going to let me tell his story. The very circumstances of their first meeting, he said, seemed to guarantee it wouldn't last. It was a night in mid-July, a chilly and rainy summer marred by upheaval and conflict. Lang had divorced his second wife that spring and there were signs that his teenage son from his first marriage was using drugs. What's more, Lang had had a tempestuous fling with his studio director, fifteen years his junior, and to cap it all he was suffering from writer's block. He had spent all summer in the city. The TV show was in hiatus, but Lang's intention had been to do a plan for the coming season: ratings were down and the network chief had made it very clear to him that a reinvention was necessary – as well as a new novel. Lang told me it was important that I understood this part: he had stayed in the city to work, not to chase women.

But even this grey, drab summer had a few evenings when the air was warm and still and thick as the sun went down. Evenings when Helsinki lay drenched in the smell of food and perfume and the sky was pale long after dusk and people exuded the scent of secrets and anticipation. Lang recounted one of these evenings for me in minute detail.

He had spent all day in his study on Villagatan, patiently stationed in front of his computer, but no ideas nor any words found their way into his head. Lang had drunk too many cups of instant cappuccino; his old stomach ulcer was starting to bother him and he was almost sick with loneliness. So at dusk he wandered down to the Corona Bar and had two bottles of smooth dark beer. A man sporting a plumed fedora was holding forth a few tables away. He was in a wheelchair and his right leg was bandaged all the way up his thigh, and Lang recognized him. He was an aging rock star who had fallen off a balcony and broken his leg and made front page news in the evening papers. Lang sat and listened to the rock star tell his admirers about Los Angeles and about his many guitars that he called "his axes". But soon Lang grew tired of his eavesdropping and wandered on to Bar 9 where he had a bowl of stir-fried chicken and noodles. When he had finished his food and a half bottle of red wine he slipped into the bar Kerma where a girl trio were singing soul songs. While they were singing Lang had two glasses of vodka and pineapple juice, later starting up a conversation with one of the singers. He praised their version of "Stand by Me" and suggested they work another Ben E. King piece into their repertoire: "I Who Have Nothing". To his surprise this woman (and she really could sing these songs, Lang remembered indignantly) had not only not heard of "I Who Have Nothing", she had never heard of Ben E. King. Lang suddenly felt old and tired and weighed down by an impenetrable layer of nostalgia trivia. He wanted to make a comeback; ask the woman if she had seen him on television, but he couldn't find the words, he was afraid she would say she didn't have a TV, that her life consisted of singing these naked old songs whose origin she didn't have a clue about. So Lang didn't say anything and the singer soon found better company. After that – Lang admitted – he had far too many more glasses of vodka and pineapple juice and when he walked the three blocks to his newly-purchased but fairly run-down one bedroom apartment on Skarpskyttegatan it was already getting light. The early morning was beautiful in a serious and quiet way, the sun a pale disc behind the clouds in the east that danced along in thin veils over the soccer field below Johannes Church, enveloping the twin spires of the church and the Ferlander House and the Industrial Art Museum only to dissolve again. Lang was struck by the beauty of his city and stopped to look, slowly sobering up in the damp early morning air. When finally he made it home, he slept until half past twelve, got up and drank half a litre of water and ate three pieces of hard tack with oily chunks of tuna fish on top. Then he spread out the morning paper and studied the TV guide, grimly noting that his network had filled the slot vacated by his ambitious literary talk show with the usual summer fare: sports, singalongs and other vacuous material.

Lang was hung over all afternoon and most of the evening. He zapped through the channels until he started to feel better and around ten o'clock he walked down to Stora Robertsgatan to get a bite to eat. He chose a simple pizzeria where you could have your individual pan pizza on a high bar stool by the window. The place was empty, but as Lang was waiting for his food, the door opened and a dark-haired woman about twenty-five years old came in. Lang watched her as she walked up to the counter and gave her order. She was slender and tall, a point underscored by her chunky platform shoes. Her face was more interesting than beautiful, looking somewhat small in proportion to her drawn-out limbs and even though the individual features were finely etched, they seemed to Lang to be somewhat incommensurable, as if the dark eyes, the small upturned nose and the broad mouth with its full bottom lip did not belong together but had been randomly assembled, as in a police sketch. Her black trousers were tight across her hips and thighs, flaring below the knees. She was wearing a purple top that was also tight and Lang couldn't help but notice that her breasts were large for all that she was so thin. Silicone or a push-up, he thought, or both.

Lang's observations were quickly coloured by his prejudices and his command of the city's social geography and by the time he and the woman were served their pizzas he had decided she was a Russian or Estonian prostitute. At this moment, as if in response to a secret signal, it began to rain. Lang dug into his pizza with gusto, cutting it into quarters and wrapping a napkin around the first piece. But the woman left hers untouched.

"Why is there no salt on the table?" she demanded, though it was not clear whom she was addressing. "Even a cheap joint like this should have a salt cellar on the table." Lang thought she was speaking Finnish with a slight accent, which reinforced his impression of her origins and profession. The woman repeated her demand for salt in a higher, shriller voice that got on his nerves.

"For the love of God," he said. "These pizzas have more than enough salt. Didn't they teach you any table manners back in Petersburg?"

"What do you mean, 'Petersburg'?" the woman said with genuine surprise. "And where's an old bastard like you from – Haparanda?"

Lang now recognized that she had no accent at all and that it was his preconceived ideas that had caused his ears to imagine one. He chose to ignore her and the grumpy cook came out and handed her the salt cellar she demanded. She scattered salt all over her Vesuvio, allowing her gaze to wander absently around the room as she did so, looking straight through Lang for a moment. Then they sat there, methodically consuming their pizzas and looking out at the street where the rain was coming down harder and was coating the flat paving slabs of the pedestrian zone with a slick wet sheen. It had, as Lang told me, been a lonely and cold summer in Helsinki and these three people – Lang, the woman and the cook – perfectly symbolized the chill that had held the city in its grip since the spring. But then something happened, because of a cosmic coincidence or because their blood-sugar levels stabilized. They softened and – simultaneously – looked up at each other. It seemed to Lang that the woman's gaze grew warm as she looked at him and he felt his own face change as one corner of his mouth was pulled up into a half-smile. Then they chorused: "You have tomato sauce on your face", and broke into the same kind of bashful laughter. When the laughter died away, the woman said, "You have to excuse me. I've had a bad day today."

And Lang said, "So have I."

The woman said, "You aren't from Haparanda, are you?"

"No. And probably you aren't from Petersburg."

"No, I'm not. I've never even been there."

"Me neither. My paternal grandfather died and my maternal granny lost her brothers in the wars. We hate Russia in our family. That is to say, I don't hate it, I just keep a respectful distance." He cringed at the banality and heavy-handed intimacy of his reply and felt his ears begin to burn. "So where *are* you from," he said in an attempt to divert attention from himself.

"From nowhere. That's what it feels like anyway. And you?"

"From here." Lang made a sweeping gesture to imply the entire city.

"I know who you are. You're Lang. I've seen you on TV."

"Christ," he said, rubbing his knuckles into his eyes.

"Don't worry," said the woman. "I don't admire you or anything. I think you interrupt your guests far too often and you sweat too much. Your face gets disgustingly shiny in the last fifteen minutes."

"Oh really," Lang said flatly and looked glumly at his last slice of pizza.

"Why don't you buy me a glass of wine, Lang," the woman said and her voice was suddenly encouraging.

"Why should I? After forty-five minutes my face is sure to get disgustingly shiny."

"Don't be silly. I see you're alone – only people who are really alone snap at strangers in restaurants. And anyway . . ."

"Anyway, what?"

She looked at him teasingly.

"I want to know if you're a better listener in real life."

When they walked out onto the street it had stopped raining. The wind had ripped a few holes in the cloud cover and planes could be seen in the darkening sky.

"You should know one thing," she said as they set off, going south-west in search of a suitable bar. "I never sleep with famous people, only with nobodies."

"That was a play on words."

"What do you mean?"

"You sleep only with those who have no bodies," Lang said.

She scowled at him and said, "I'm starting to think you're better on TV after all."

"Fifteen-love."

She wasn't lying, at least not about first dates: she slept on Lang's sofa and he wasn't allowed so much as a kiss. When he tried, she gently but firmly restrained him. How Lang fared as a listener, naturally he couldn't judge, but he did find out a great deal about her even then: how her family had moved around during her childhood so she had never settled anywhere, how they had ended up in Helsinki when she was sixteen and how she had graduated from a high school in an out-lying suburb a few years later. How she had applied to the Institute of Dramatic Arts but had lost out at the final phase and how she had thereafter studied psychology and literature and such like at the university, but tired of that after a few years. She told him that she had first heard his name in a seminar on Contemporary Finnish Literature; one of her classmates had written an essay on the influence on Lang's work of Jean-Henri Quedec's theory of the simulatory subject paradox of the double being. It was that very essay, she told him, that convinced her that literature was the last thing she wanted to devote herself to. By this time she had long since pulled off her purple shirt, revealing the skimpiest white tank top beneath and when Lang at an earlier point had stood up to go to the kitchen for another bottle of wine he had walked behind the sofa where she sat leaning slightly forward and caught sight of an expanse of skin and spine in the faint morning light that was already seeping in through the window. With the image of that naked back still engraved on his retina Lang declared that he was ashamed of having spent his entire adult life on such abstract and life-denying things as writing books and talking to people on TV. She looked sceptically at him and then said very seriously, "You're looking at me as if I were a sculpture. I think you are such an aesthete it's hard for you to be human." Lang was knocked off balance and couldn't find a single word to say in reply. "We have already spent several hours together. I'm sitting on your sofa, drinking your wine and you haven't even asked me my name. I'm Sarita."

"I'm Christian," Lang said unnecessarily. "But of course you know that. My friends call me Kride."

"You have friends?"

Lang didn't reply. He didn't know what to say. She made him unsure of himself. Because he didn't say anything, Sarita started talking, telling him about her son Miro who was going to turn six and who was spending the summer with his grandmother in Virdois. She also told him that she had worked as a research editor for an interview programme for a TV network, not the one Lang worked for, but that she was currently working as an assistant to a fashion photographer, and eventually she said she was getting tired and would like to sleep for a few hours on Lang's sofa. Lang wanted to ask her why she had given up an intellectually stimulating research position for the shallow world of fashion; he wanted to ask her where she lived and who Miro's father was, but instead he asked, "How old are you?" To which she answered, "I have several ages. Which one do you want?" Lang said good night and went to his bedroom where he tossed and turned in his bed, switching sides several times, sweating and cursing his decision to brew strong coffee after they came up from the bar. He got up and walked out into the living room. Sarita was asleep; she had already managed to kick off the blanket he had brought out for her. Lang sat back down in the chair he had been sitting in earlier, looked at her half-open mouth and the collection of different-coloured bracelets on her right wrist. And he looked at the dark hair that fanned out across the sofa cushion and her deep navel that rose and sank with her breath. Even then, he said to me later, he knew very well what was going to happen.

III

By the time Lang got up Sarita was gone. There was no note. It was sunny outside, but when he checked through the kitchen window he saw an approaching cold front chasing crisp-edged fluffy clouds high up in the sky. He walked down to a café bakery by Femkanten and bought a croissant and a sandwich. The young woman behind the counter looked at him conspiratorially and smiled shyly, as if Lang's fame was their little secret. He asked for the items to be bagged, took them home, made coffee and had his breakfast. When he finished, he showered, then stood in front of the mirror and grimaced at his naked chest. Lang was in relatively good condition and was careful to follow a sensible, low-fat diet and even so his age was showing. His face had lost its sharp outlines after the two sleepless nights; his eyes were tired and swollen. Here and there the skin was starting to droop and exercise could do nothing to arrest that process.

While Lang studied himself in the mirror it dawned on him that Sarita had not left her phone number, that he didn't know her last name and that he had no idea where she lived: he had let her disappear without trace. He pulled on a pair of black cycling shorts, a windproof sport jacket, his air cushion trainers and then walked into the courtyard to get his bike from the storage shed. He cycled out through the gate, turning down towards Femkanten following the narrow Sjömansgatan down to the West harbour. He took the road through Gräsviken, past the doomed Lepakko building and out towards Drumsö Island. Keeping to the right side of the island, he cycled across bridges to Svedjeholmen and Lövö Island not caring that the cold wind made him came out in goose pimples. From Lövo Island he turned back to the city, clenching his teeth in the easterly wind and occasionally giving a passing motorist the finger, muttering: damn this summer.

Back at Villagatan he locked up his bike, walked into the stale-smelling office and turned on the computer. But the endorphin rush he usually felt after a bike ride did not kick in. Lang stared despondently at the screen and didn't even notice when the screen saver came on, only hearing Sarita's voice in his head: *You have friends?* and *I have several ages, which one do you want?* But he had already forgotten, he admitted to me later, that she had accused him of being an aesthete who looked at her as if she were a sculpture. Staring at the screen saver's slowly rotating geometric figures he recalled the delicate impression of her spine in the soft morning light, he saw the different-coloured bracelets around her sleep-heavy wrist, and he saw her deep navel rise and fall in time with her breath.

Over the next few weeks Lang took long bike rides every day, letting his mind drift among the geometric figures and endless space of the computer screen when he was done. His son was in London for the summer and neither of his ex-wives nor his studio director lover would have anything to do with him, and his nearly seventy-five-year-old mother had gone to Lake Garda with the Hagalund retired people's association. Lang had no duties and no people to see. The city was empty of people, half-asleep in its wait for the winter residents to return. To Lang it had come to seem foreign and ageless.

One unusually warm and sunny Thursday he biked to Ingå and back, a ride of some 120 kilometres. He made it back to Helsinki after midnight. Crossing Drumsö bridge the night air felt to him like velvet, but already within the warm air that smelled of seaweed and wild roses and petrol he could sense the advancing chill and desolation of autumn. After this strenuous ride Lang developed an inflammation in the calf muscles of both legs. He bought two enormous tubes of Mobilat, massaging the lotion into his legs morning and night and discovering that it boosted his masculinity: he felt like a warrior or a professional athlete, standing there in his dark kitchen working the ointment into his aching limbs.

Lang devoted his evenings to finding Sarita. He had called all of the fashion photographers he knew, and when none of them remembered working with a Sarita he began instead to look in the area where he had met her. One night he wandered in and out of the bars on Nyland street, having a glass of pineapple juice in each one and only switching to almond liqueur when his bladder signalled defeat. The following evening he combed the Boulevard, moving between Tony's Deli in the north and Bulevardia in the south, making small forays into Annegatan, Fredriksgatan and Eriksgatan. The day after that it was Stora Robertsgatan and its array of joints, then Skillnaden and the Esplanades, then – and by this time it was Friday, so he had to wait in line before being allowed in – he toured Alexandersgatan, the City Passage and the Glass Palace.

And so it went, day after day, week after week. Lang tired of pineapple juice and of almond liqueur. By the middle of August he had polished off two whole areas of the city: Främre Tölö and Kronohagen, and he had crossed Långa Bron Bridge and looked for Sarita in the taverns on Berghäll. Lang now returned to downtown. He thought about the proud way she carried herself and he was convinced she had a past as a model, despite her irregular features, and he knew that models for the most part favoured the trendy bars in the city centre, the ones with big plate glass windows to show off the clientele. He started asking friends and bar acquaintances if they had seen anyone who matched Sarita's description. One evening he slunk into the House of Bourbon on the corner of Nyland and Albertsgatan – he was a regular there and had even played in celebrity soccer matches for charity with the bartender (and former schlager singer) Vekku. While Vekku polished glasses behind the bar, Lang leaned against the dark wood-panelled counter and tried to describe Sarita's face, its smallness and the extraordinary, oddly-proportioned way of her eyes and nose and mouth. It was Tuesday evening, the sun was going down and the bar was almost empty and Vekku said, "You really want to find her, don't you?" and Lang who was just about to launch further into his description of her, stopped himself and said with surprise "Yes, as a matter of fact, I do."

"What makes her so special?"

"I don't know. I've only met her once. She doesn't say things you'd expect."

Vekku carefully finished drying a glass, put it down, then picked up another which he also started to polish. He shook his shaved head and said, "I'll keep my eyes and ears open, Lang. That's all I can promise."

Even during these weeks, Lang admitted to me, he sensed that his interest in her was changing to desire and obsession. He had taken no part in the Helsinki night scene for many years, ever since the books and above all the TV show had made him so well-known that he had grown skittish in public, startled by people shouting "Hey, Lang!" and total strangers wanting to discuss the latest show with him. Lang had also run into young men who shouted "Fucking Jew!" at him – it happened that people confused him with Ruben Stiller of the talk show "Stiller" – and once a drunken hockey player confused him with Timo Harakka from the "Black Box" show (Harakka had a past as a left-leaning activist), but that was hardly a comfort.

Now Lang was forced to overcome his apprehension and an inner compulsion drove him out into the city night after night. Every week he accepted the back-slapping and the insults from the Helsinki party crowd, smiling absently, nodding and then making his way over to the counter where he would describe Sarita to the bartender and the table staff. Each time Lang waited with the same sense of anticipation while they racked their brains with thoughtful expressions and he felt his hope and desire produce a sensation of fluttering in his chest and stomach. It was like waking up after hibernation, it even hurt a little, as when you lie on your arm in bed and it falls asleep and then the blood starts to circulate again in spurts.

But his investigations always ended the same way: everyone was sorry and they shook their heads no. So it was that Lang had more or less given up when one day there was a text message on the green display of his mobile: "Has this been the summer of our discontent?" Lang later claimed to have paid no attention to this first message. His phone number was secret and his producer, the TV network and his publishers worked as a kind of filter for him. But sometimes the filter leaked and Lang had had to listen both to propositions as well as threats. He was therefore more thick-skinned by this time. But the following morning the message "What did Raphael do when he painted La Fornarina?" awakened his curiosity, his mind started to spin, he formulated a suspicion about the identity of the sender and after a brief hesitation he rang the number. An anonymous male voice said, "The party you have tried to reach is unavailable. You may leave a message after the tone." The note was long and high-pitched and when it finally stopped Lang said, "I don't even know if this is who I think it is – but I suppose that Raphael slept with her." He paused for a second or two then added: "I've been looking for you."

IIII

A few days later Lang stood shivering outside an apartment building on Helsingegatan. Sarita hadn't wanted to give him the entry code and so he had to wait outside for quite a while. He stamped his feet in the clear but chilly evening air while a steady stream of people went by. A young man with cropped hair and sharp eyes slowed down as he approached Lang, passing him slowly and then turning around to give him a searching look. Lang assumed he was sizing him up as a potential customer, someone interested in the small drug stash he no doubt carried under his coat. Lang looked deliberately away and turned up the collar of his leather jacket.

At last Sarita came down and opened the door, dressed in a thick white wool jumper and a flowing knee-length skirt. The skirt was made out of crepe-like material and produced a frothy sound as she walked him to the lift.

"Where did you look for me?" she said.

Lang told her.

"I never go to those places," she said. "I just happened to be at that pizzeria. I had spent all day at the library on Richardsgatan."

"What were you doing there?" Lang said.

"Reading."

"What were you reading?"

"I don't remember," Sarita said, and Lang had the feeling she wasn't telling the truth. "Maybe a book by Celati or Chekhov. Or perhaps I wasn't reading at all, just thinking. I do that sometimes – go to churches or libraries and think. They're good places to gather your thoughts, don't you find?"

Lang didn't answer; he tried to remember the last time he visited a library or a church, but could only establish that it must have been a long time ago. The lift groaned in an alarming way and when it passed the fourth floor they heard a woman shout, "Go on, just leave! Go to that fucking slut of yours!" and a man's voice said, "Do you always have to get so hysterical? Can't we argue without you starting to cry?" Lang and Sarita looked at each other in an embarrassed way and Sarita said, "She's pregnant and he's met someone else. They're always arguing. But I can't hear them from inside my apartment."

Sarita had a big one-bedroom apartment with windows facing towards the courtyard. There was no hall or entry way; you stepped right into the living room. The wall between the kitchen and the living room had been removed creating an open-plan living area. In an alcove in the front corner there was a child's bed, a dresser and on the floor there were a few plastic dinosaurs and a radio-controlled Nikko car. Closer to the kitchen end, in front of a large window, there was a small sofa and over by the opposite wall there was a new TV set and next to it was a brand-new video recorder that had not yet been unpacked from its box. The TV was set at an angle in such a way that it could be watched either from the sofa or the child's bed. In the kitchen there was a little table with three somewhat rickety bistro chairs. The walls were white and bare except for a framed Magritte poster and one of Cartier-Bresson's classic photographs, enormously enlarged, of a Parisian boulevard in the rain.

"Paris is a wonderful city," Lang said, attempting conversation.

"I've never been there."

"Is your boy still in the country?"

"Miro is coming back in a few days," Sarita said. She pushed open the door to the bedroom and two cats slunk out, one with long grey fur, the other short-haired, black, with yellow eyes.

"I'm a dog-person," Lang said. "Cats make me nervous."

"Then you'll get along fine. Both Noa and Dmitri are afraid of men."

"How do they like your bo– Miro?" Lang said, correcting himself.

"They're not actually mine. I'm looking after them for a friend who's spending the summer in Madrid. She helps me with Miro during the winter so I promised to help out with her cats."

She opened a kitchen cupboard and started taking out plates and glasses.

"Which one is Dmitri and which one Noa?" Lang said.

"Dmitri is the black one," Sarita said. "They're both castrated."

While she was preparing dinner, Lang went into the bedroom. It was a small room dominated by the wide bed. Next to the bed there was a make-up table with bottles and jars. On the floor between the bed and the window was a ghetto blaster, and some CD cases lay strewn about. The walls were bare and the room felt as cold and uninhabited as the rest of the apartment.

"How long have you lived here?" Lang shouted to Sarita, who had just turned on the water on the other side of the wall.

"Since the beginning of June," she shouted back. "We lived in Karbole before that, Miro and I. Marko found this for us. One of his friends owns it."

"Who is Marko?"

"Miro's father."

Lang bent down and picked up the CDs. The artists didn't mean anything to him, and he put them down on the mirror table. He caught sight of a photo stuck between the mirror and the frame and leaned in to get a closer look. A very young Sarita was in the picture. She had a wide smile and her hair had a different, reddish cast to it. She held a blond toddler of about one or one and a half in her arms. He was grumpy. A young man stood next to her, on her right. He held his arm around her, but his expression was closed and serious. He wore his hair in a ponytail, had hard eyes and Lang had to admit he was handsome, strikingly more so than Lang. Marko, he thought and at once the man looked familiar. Possibly Lang had met him during the weeks he had spent looking for Sarita in the city's bars, clubs and pubs.

Sarita had made a seafood quiche, as well as a salad with roast beef and sun-dried tomatoes. The wine Lang had brought was heavy, with vanilla and liquorice notes. Gradually Lang warmed up inside, waking up – he told me – from the loneliness of that summer. He softened throughout his entire body, kindling to the idea that he was actually *with* someone, and not simply *someone*: Sarita, the woman he had been looking for for a month. Their hands touched already at the beginning of the meal, Lang told me, and when the bottle of wine was finished Sarita got up – not to get another, but to carefully and without a fuss take Lang's hand in hers and interlace her fingers with his. They went to her bedroom and Lang closed the door in Dmitri's face. Then they stood in the middle of the floor and embraced each other in the dark. After a while Sarita pulled away, kneeled down and looked for one of the CD albums that had been lying on the floor.

"I put them on the table," Lang said, holding his breath so she wouldn't notice how heavily and unevenly he was breathing. Sarita got up, passing him with only a few centimetres between them. Her breathing seemed to Lang to be completely relaxed and smooth. She touched his thigh lightly then grabbed the CDs, going back to the ghetto blaster and hesitating. Lang used the time to take his clothes off and get under the covers. He had not been to bed with anyone since the beginning of June and wanted to skip the undressing. A fifteen-year-old struggling with clasps and buttons might be touching, he said to me, but a forty-year-old talk show host who does the same would hardly score any points.

The music Sarita put on was serious and beautiful. It was a woman singer with an ethereal but also raw-edged voice. The piece had a lonely, echoing quality that Lang had a special weakness for. Sarita took her clothes off. She didn't turn her back but stood facing Lang the whole time, then she walked to the bed, climbed in and calmly threw back the covers. She lay down close to Lang and put her hand on his stomach, letting her long nails glide over his skin. But Lang was far from relaxed. His shoulders were tight and his heart was pounding, not from desire but from desire mixed with fear. He kept imagining a key turning in the lock at the front door and an athletic young man with a ponytail and hard gaze walking in, coming to the side of Sarita's bed ready to smash Lang to pieces.

"Look how tense you are," Sarita said. "What is it?"

Lang didn't answer, and noticed too late that Sarita was watching him in the dim light and that he had allowed his gaze instinctively to fall on the picture on the dressing table.

"Are you afraid of Marko?"

Lang didn't say anything.

"Don't worry," Sarita said. "He doesn't have a key to this place. We've been divorced for a long time." Then she softly placed her hand over his eyes. Obediently he closed them. He felt her put her head on his shoulder and then after a while he was able to relax.

*

Lang had said to me how for years he had been amazed at how the most disparate thoughts and phrases seemed to lie in wait under the surface of the brain only to appear at the most strange times. This time it was a phrase he attributed to Jean-Paul Sartre, but he wasn't altogether sure. Some time during his years of study Lang had memorized this phrase in English and now it flashed up in his mind like the part title of a silent film: it came to him when Sarita lay beneath him and they had both started moaning and breathing fast and she was digging her nails into the small of his back and buttocks as if to spur him on. In Lang's consciousness the phrase blended with the music and lyrics of the CD that was now playing for the second time. *By becoming a part of the uniqueness of our time, we finally merge with the eternal*, the Sartre part title proclaimed, but in the bedroom the music echoed all around them and the woman with the raw but ethereal voice sang the words "don't waste your breath, don't waste your heart", and the moonlight that found its way in through the window was ghostly and pale and in that moment Lang's muddled mind and newly wakened senses forged a new maxim:

By becoming a part of the uniqueness of our time
we waste our breath and waste our heart.

And then Lang opened his eyes and met Sarita's gaze which was locked on his face. Her eyes were wide open and Lang thought he could see ideas and emotions moving in them like waves on the ocean. He saw pleasure but also unspoken questions in the midst of the pleasure: fear, strength and suspicion, and longing, ridicule and pity, and much more.

V

Something inside him burst that first night with Sarita, Lang confessed, something that made him give in to feelings he had long kept at bay.

Lang had always kept a finger on the pulse of contemporary society, and would argue that this sensitivity to trends was his strongest weapon in the struggle for a comfortable existence. He had made the necessary adjustment from a vague, antiquated leftism to a cosmopolitan consumerism even during Ronald Reagan's first presidency. At that time many of his friends, me included, amused ourselves with coming up with bad jokes about Reagan and Margaret Thatcher and the impending downfall of global capitalism. Lang's novels had from the outset been labyrinthine and free of traditional chronology and he had quickly become a favourite of the leading intellectuals. He was seen as the fast-moving, post-modern prize catch in the muddy sea of Nordic realism, where I made up a part of the nitrogen surplus. Later, he had also gained popularity through his move to television. Those of us close to Lang knew him to be an internally conflicted person, but in the eye of the camera and spotlights he seemed to cohere into a smooth whole, an appealing blend of yin and yang. On the TV screen the usually somewhat chilly and laconic Lang exuded an ideal combination of warmth, charm and intellectual rigour. Lang combined the hard-edged self-consciousness of hosts such as Sarasvuo, Stiller and Harakka with the empathy and intuition of his female peers such as Tastula and Pyykko, and the result was that "Sininen Hetki", "The Blue Hour", was both compelling and challenging, a show that reigned as the number one talk show season after season.

But the summer he met Sarita – or more precisely for much of the previous year – Lang had more and more often come to feel exhausted and somehow thinned-out. He told me it had become even harder for him to meet people, or rather, not harder but more devoid of meaning, as if deep inside he knew that regardless of whether he visited his aging mother, invited his teenage son for dinner, had lunch with one of his ex-wives or slept with some young woman he met in a bar, there were no real exchanges between people any more. Everything had turned into a soap opera by a mediocre writer; a predictable mish-mash of undeveloped characters and tired, clichéd dialogue. Increasingly Lang felt a violent sadness well up inside him, a lump in his throat and a tightening in his gut with no obvious cause. When spring had arrived he had registered the newly awakened city's still unclothed beauty and he had always admired its rare white evening light that made the Art Nouveau buildings of the Ulrikasborg and Eira districts shimmer like fairy-tale palaces. But this spring Lang's soul had remained empty and dead in spite of the surrounding beauty and for the first time in his life he found Helsinki's appearance stark and unfriendly, as if there were something frozen and repressive about the multitude of green and black rooftops, spires and towers of the old city, as if the city lay closed like an oyster around its forgotten history. He had felt an unexplained urge to cry, Lang said, it was as if the Nordic spring and everything coming back to life was draining his already diminished will to live, as if the light was speaking directly to

27

repressed feelings within him and at the same time taunted him for his weakness and lack of courage. But courage to do what? Lang had asked, and he had done everything he could to conceal his crumbling centre from the world. He had meetings with his producer, his publishers, he had stayed up nights to jump-start his new book, and he had undertaken the last round of shows with his usual intensity, without revealing any of the weakness or insecurity he felt. He had given interviews to the press and even worked on "Talk about News" as the poet Tabermann's sidekick. And through all this, Lang said, he had been able to maintain his mask of cordiality and wit. But when summer rolled around with a yawning calendar and a release from his usual duties the signs of fatigue became so pronounced that Lang could no longer ignore them. He slept nine hours a night but had no desire to get up when the alarm went off. He stopped answering calls, turned off his mobile and let the messages accumulate in his voice mail. By July he found it hard to open the envelopes that came in the post − he was afraid of what he would find in them and the remarkable thing, he said, was that praise was now as painful to his ears as criticism − and he had not logged in to his e-mail in nearly a month. And then, during the long, lonely weeks when he sat in front of his computer, took long cycle rides and looked for Sarita, Lang's senses started deceiving him. He started to exhibit signs of paranoia. As he moved from bar to bar in his search for Sarita he imagined that he heard someone whisper: "There goes Lang − but how wasted and tired he looks!" and "Lang can't take the pressure any more. He's lost his grip." And a third voice added, "Didn't his ratings fall drastically this winter?" Lang started to run from these voices. He fled into the image fragments and short bits of music that had began to haunt his mind that spring and summer, old flotsam, snatches of images from his childhood and early adolescence involving his father, mother, his big sister, friends and all the girls he had ever fallen in love with. But sometimes the people were so unfamiliar and the scenes and the music so strange that Lang could no longer say with any certainty if these were his own legitimate memories or scenes from some film he had seen long ago.

After that first night with Sarita, Lang went from being largely silent to something of a chatterbox, lost in nostalgic reverie. At two o'clock in the morning they got up out of bed, wrapped themselves in blankets and sat down at the kitchen table. While they drank calvados and ate some cheesecake that Sarita had bought at the supermarket, Lang told her about a time long ago when money could not be had from machines in the wall, but you had to get to the bank before four o'clock or there you were without any purchasing power, since credit cards and cheques were only for the rich. And he talked about what it was like keeping in touch with people before the days of answering machines and e-mail and mobiles. He told her about how people simply didn't answer the phone, were not accessible and how you had to wait for days – perhaps even weeks or months – before they returned from their travels.

"We have become so spoiled and insensitive," he preached for Sarita. "Everything has to happen now. We don't wait for anyone or anything. We respect no-one. Other people are simply a product we may or may not have use for."

"Yes," Sarita said dryly. "They look good as guests in a talk show, for example."

Later, when they had gone back to the bedroom and rain had started drumming monotonously against the windowpane, Lang told her about a summer a long time ago when he shared an apartment with a school friend who was working as a piano mover over the holidays and who in the evenings wore a pale yellow Lacoste shirt that was much too small for him and who went to the disco at the Finnish School of Business to chase girls who smeared their lips with pink lip gloss. He talked about the thick brown envelopes that he and the friend – that was me – got at the end of every month and about the great joy of having moved from home. We had rented a one-bedroom apartment together that summer, Lang and I, the summer after we graduated from high school. He talked about the joy of being his own master and getting his own *liksa*.

"Liksa?" Sarita said, tasting the word. "What was in those envelopes anyway?"

"Cash," Lang said, smiling happily at the memory. "A thick wad of delicious, rustling bank notes."

"Oh, money," Sarita said. "Of course. What an idiot I am."

"How can you say that? You aren't an idiot," Lang said tenderly. They had made love again and he felt as warm and smug as a cat.

"I suspect you are actually much smarter than me," he said.

"Oh no you don't," she said. "You're smart, Lang, you're as smart as the devil, don't try to get me to think anything else."

"I'm not smart at all," Lang said. "I'm tired, I'm so terribly tired."

"I know you are," Sarita said. "I can hear it in your voice. It's like a fire that's about to go out." She met his look of surprise and went on, "You feel out of step with the world and it makes you sad and afraid because it was precisely your ability to stay in tune with the present that made you think you were eternally young and forever able to reinvent yourself."

Lang looked at Sarita with something approaching dread. Sartre! he thought. She can read my thoughts. She read that flash card in my head. There's something frightening about her. But he said nothing. Instead she was the one who continued to talk. She lay next to him, propped up on one elbow and let her fingers get tangled in the hair on his chest, and she said: "You're afraid of death, Lang. And there's nothing wrong with that. When you've come that far you've managed to rid yourself of a lot of other illusions and then when you aren't afraid of anything else except death you can start working on the most important thing."

"And what's that?" Lang asked, his heart beating violently.

"To learn not to be afraid of death," Sarita said. "Because that's like learning to die, and learning to die is the same as learning to live."

"Don't say that!" Lang said sharply.

"Why not?" Sarita said and calmly met his look of consternation.

"I don't want to think about things like that!"

"No," Sarita said teasingly. "You only want to think about my firm young flesh."

"Well, why not?" Lang said. "I'm like any other man, damn it, and I certainly don't want to face up to any truths." He was quiet for a few seconds, then said, "We're all afraid of the truth."

And it was then that Sarita said the words that were like a lullaby to his ears.

"Don't you worry," she said. "Don't worry yourself about it, my tired Lang. Let yourself rest a little. Rest here next to me."

Those words, Lang later told me, broke down the last of his resistance. He felt the unexplained sorrow well up inside him and this time he didn't fight it; he hid his face in Sarita's neck and cried. Not very much, and quietly, but still. And the strangest thing, Lang said, was that when he finally allowed himself to cry, even though it was only a little, then the familiar sorrow suddenly felt like something else: it almost felt like happiness and life.

While the darkness slowly broke up around them and was replaced by a grey and rainy day, Lang and Sarita lay face to face, their arms around each other, awake but silent. When Lang closed his eyes he saw some of those image fragments that haunted him, but he didn't want to tell me which ones they were. That wasn't the point, he said, the point was that when he lay there in the warmth of Sarita's arms those pictures didn't hurt as they usually did, they were just there in his head and that was that. And then Lang gradually felt his desire for her return, it was already a spent and exhausted desire but desire nonetheless. Sarita answered his careful caresses and then they made love again, this time without haste and with a hunger that was gentle and almost tender. And it was now that she said his name in the way that he was going to learn to thirst for. The whole thing had a fairly banal explanation. She whispered his first name, but her tongue could not quite get around the hard t-sound between the s and the i. She didn't say Christian, but instead she whispered again and again: Chrisshan, my Chrisshan. Don't worry about it, Chrisshan. And it was at this point, Lang said, that he could no longer deny to himself he was in love. And he sensed that he would one day come to tell her about the images that haunted him, about the memories of his sister Estelle the winter she became sick and the memories of his father silent and stern at his desk in the living room on Petersgatan and about all the other memories he had never told anyone and never even been able to put down in words and thereby neutralize.

VI

Lang stayed in the apartment on Helsingegatan for three days. Every morning he accompanied Sarita as she took the number 8 tram to the fashion photographer's studio that was in a converted factory building on Repslagargatan. Then Lang dutifully made his way to his office on Villagatan where he pretended to work, and mostly thought about how he wanted to see Sarita again. On the morning of the third day he went to his apartment to get a change of clothes. There were eleven calls on the answering machine which he listened to, then returned a few of them. One person he called was his producer, a dynamic man by the name of V.P. Minkkinen who had his own production company, a shaved head and a taste for anorexically-thin women.

"We have a problem, Lang," Minkkinen said. "The network execs are starting to think we're too expensive. We should put our heads together some time, see what we can come up with."

"It'll have to wait until the second week of September," Lang said. "I'm on holiday until then, or rather," he lied, "I'm working on something else until then."

"I'm not sure our bosses will wait that long," Minkkinen said with a deceptively mild tone of voice.

"They'll just have to," Lang said firmly and hung up. Then he wrapped his electric toothbrush and a strip of ulcer pills in a paper towel, slipped them into the inner pocket of his linen jacket, went to the corner store and bought a packet of frozen crayfish. He walked back to Sarita's apartment, letting himself in with the key she had given him and dumped the crayfish into a bucket, putting it into the sink with lukewarm water. He got the impression Sarita had been home during the day: there was a cup and a plate on the counter that he didn't remember from the morning, and the lamp over the kitchen table was on even though he was almost sure he had turned it off when he left. Maybe, Lang thought as he walked into the bedroom and lay down on her bed, she had come home and had a bite to eat before she went to the station to pick up her son. He was arriving on the three o'clock train from Tampere, travelling all alone which Lang thought strange given that the boy was only six.

Lang was in the apartment when Sarita arrived with Miro. It was not, Lang said dryly to me later, a good first meeting. He was introduced as Chrisshan-setä, Uncle Christian, but this time Sarita's soft pronunciation didn't have any effect. Miro looked up at him, then his bottom lip started to tremble and the boy began to cry as softly as Lang had cried in Sarita's bed two and a half days earlier. Miro had gone to his little corner, and squeezed the Nikko car to his chest as if it were a talisman that could ward off the evil wizard Lang.

"Where is Marko-daddy?" he asked. Sarita threw a quick glance at Lang, then answered,

"I don't know, Miro. I honestly don't know. Maybe in Tallinn."

"Where's Tallinn?"

"In Estonia," Sarita answered. "You'll get to see him soon, Miro, I promise."

Miro liked the crayfish even though they were still half-frozen. Lang patiently kept him supplied with meat from the tails and claws he peeled and the boy ate eagerly without warming to Lang himself. When Lang asked him well-meaning questions Miro ignored him, with a distant, truculent expression on his face. Sarita also appreciated the crayfish. She slurped and smacked her way through them, drinking heroically of the Chardonnay, and Lang noted that she was one of those who not only ate the tail, but sucked on the head and the abdomen. But neither the crayfish nor the wine helped; that night Sarita refused to sleep with him. He tried to caress the inside of her thigh, but she carefully removed his hand and said she didn't want Miro to be woken by the sounds of lovemaking on the first night he was back. Lang had the vague sense that Miro was only an excuse, that something else was bothering her. He imagined that Miro's return had reminded her of who she was, and for a few moments he felt uncomfortable and superfluous in her bed. But then Sarita slipped down along his chest and stomach. For a second Lang felt her lips against his navel. She raised herself up on her elbows, moving her head back and forth so her long hair tickled his skin. She put one hand on the left side of his groin, letting it trail down the inside of his thigh and then back up until she softly touched his member. Then she brought her hand up to his mouth, laid her index finger over his lips and said "sssshhhh". Lang bit her finger gently. A little later she slid back up again, pressing her whole body into his, kissing him and trying to pass something into his mouth.

"Don't do that," Lang said abruptly.

"Why not?" Sarita giggled playfully in his ear. "It's only a part of you."

"I'm not doing this," he said in a low voice. "I've been in this situation before. You think there's something humiliating about what you just did and now you want to transfer that feeling onto me by spitting my own sperm into my mouth. It's silly."

Sarita pulled back from him and looked both surprised and angry. She pursed her lips and let his semen drip onto his stomach, then she turned over on her back and draped a leg over him so that her foot nudged his genitals.

"My turn," she whispered. "My turn, my smart, smart Lang."

"What about Miro?" Lang asked.

"I'm going to be quiet," Sarita said. "As quiet as you."

The next day it was Friday and Sarita and Miro were leaving to spend the weekend with Miro's godmother, a hair stylist called Kirsi, who had inherited a cabin in the Heinola area. Lang had left the apartment in the morning after fruitless attempts at conversation with Miro at the breakfast table. Miro was still not interested. He glared and gave one-word answers to all of Lang's questions.

Lang immediately took the necessary measures, he later admitted, to restore his independence, his cool and his ability to think clearly. He was, he confessed, a fearful person, afraid of many things and among those intimacy, and now he had – impractically enough – gone and fallen in love with Sarita. And since it was the last weekend in August he had a ready-made, already arranged way to do this: the yearly sailing jaunt with Uncle Harry, who was actually not his uncle but his mother's cousin.

Uncle Harry was sixteen years younger than Lang's mother. He had a few years left to go to sixty, but was already white-haired and had the sharp, eagle-like, weathered profile that a few lucky men acquire as they get older. Harry was an engineer and worked as the head of his department at Nokia. He had married fairly late in life and was childless even though his wife was much younger than he was. In his earliest youth, Lang – he admitted this without demur – had been a committed anarchist, full of prejudice. He felt justified in his opinion that engineers were soul- and heartless and he had at that time only the most fleeting relationship with Uncle

Harry. Lang could not even remember when and where they became friends, all he knew was that they had grown closer over the years and that sometimes he sensed that Harry had become a stand-in for the father Lang no longer had.

Lang had served fifteen summers as a hand on Uncle Harry's boat. It was every year the last Friday in August when he took the train from Helsinki to Hango. He had an enormous duffel bag slung over his shoulder, there were always storm warnings and when Lang wandered down from the station to the harbour he always hummed the words from the well-known children's song – ". . . a seaman's sack for dad, a Sunday dress for mom . . ." – because he knew he was something of a substitute for the son Harry had never had. Harry gave his orders clearly and calmly, fully expecting to be obeyed. At first Lang had laughed at him. He had been twenty-five years old.

"Why are you laughing?" Harry had asked as they sailed over the rough Vidskar Bay.

"Because you actually expect to be obeyed, don't you?"

"What's so funny about that?" Harry had asked.

"This is just a game," Lang had replied. "Not a military manoeuvre, or anything like that. I can sit with my arms folded, or get off anytime I like."

"Be my guest," Harry said and made a sweeping gesture out to the green, frothy water.

"That's not what I mean," Lang had said. "I'm just surprised you seem to think that there's any fundamental structure left which is worthy of respect."

"But there is," Harry had replied. "It's just that we seldom notice it."

Lang had held his tongue at this point, but he had refused to make his way across the slippery deck to the prow and the spinnaker.

"Nothing is a game," Harry had said. "Or else everything is a game, including military manoeuvres, the corporations where we work, and the like. But the wind can pick up even more, we could be in for a storm, and we are some kind of friends you and I, but we also have a long way to sail and we could both die – is your freedom worth that?"

Lang still said nothing.

"Come on, get to it," Harry had said. "The storm is on its way. I can hear it."

"I can't hear anything," Lang had muttered in a surly voice.

Harry had smiled and said, "It's not a sound you can hear, it's something you feel, and it takes years to develop the ability."

They set up camp in the same places year after year. The first night they always pulled into a lagoon in the area of the archipelago beyond Hitis. There was always a strong wind and beyond the shoreline boulders – that were smooth and softly rounded as reclining women's breasts which have not yet been pumped up with silicone – the wind tore at the pine trees, it whined across the pockets of wilting wild flowers and carelessly tossed seaweed up into the crevasses between the rocks.

Lang claimed that Uncle Harry had an exceptionally rational mind. He could navigate through the night and make complicated calculations based on the position of the stars. He never forgot to put the provisions away and secure the remaining belongings when the wind picked up. Even after sinking the most incredible amounts of alcohol, Harry could still explain the intricate challenges in European telecommunications or describe the last annual meeting of the Society of Finnish Engineers in minute detail. For the most part, however, Harry and Lang talked about women. Once they had finished the wine and half a bottle of whisky this was always the topic they turned to. Although if truth be told, Lang said, Harry would get out a telescope and start studying the night sky while it was Lang with his incessant talking who disturbed the scene with its wind, the stars and the silence that had settled between them.

"I think I have found the Pleiades," Harry interrupted him that year as Lang was disjointedly relating the new affair with Sarita.

"Why does her voice become cooler every time she understands how crazy I am about her? Can you explain that?" Lang said, refusing to be curtailed.

"I can't," Harry said brusquely.

"Of course you can, you know everything," Lang teased. He was already pretty drunk.

"She probably feeds on the insecurity; you have a liking for that yourself, you know. But now you have to stop talking for a while."

"Why?" Lang said.

"Because we can never become real friends if you're always going to be so afraid of silence between us," Harry said kindly. Lang went down into the cabin and returned to the cockpit with a bottle of gin.

"I bought this before I got on the train."

"Ummm," Harry said distantly.

Then Lang sat and looked at the stars for a long time, listening to the wind and drinking the bitter, undiluted spirits.

"Why can I only love in the wrong way?" he said later that night. "Do you know the answer, Harry?"

Even as he posed the question, he thought: here I am, forty years old and asking for fatherly advice. I ask questions like this last one and there's something the matter with me.

"How do you mean 'the wrong way'?" Harry wondered. "Do you mean the wrong person?"

"No, the wrong way," Lang said.

"What do you mean 'the wrong way'?" Harry was starting to

get irritated with him because it was clear that Lang had drunk far too much.

"In an unrealistic way," Lang mumbled. "In a fantasy-land kind of way."

"I don't understand the kind of questions you're asking this year," Harry said in a milder tone of voice.

"Of course you do," Lang slurred. "You understand everything."

"Not women, not men, not people," Harry said and turned his telescope back to the night sky. "I don't understand all that."

Lang admitted to me that he drank way too much that night. In the early hours of the morning he woke up in his bunk and threw up in the slop bucket. Afterwards he crawled on deck to empty it out. The stars were fading from the sky, the wind moaned over the low island rocks and the surface of the black water in the lagoon was rippled by small, chilly crests. Lang stood on deck for a long time. He had a hangover and felt awful. He thought that there was nothing more pathetic than a middle-aged, successful man who still had a teenager inside, but a teenager who interpreted his whole life as a story of suffering and who remembered only darkness where there had clearly been sun.

"It's always August," Lang thought as he stood there alone in the early morning. "Summer is always at an end and the weather is clear, but there are storms, and Uncle Harry gets less and less talkative every year and I become a better and better ship's hand, but I will never get life worked out and the storms will keep on coming and I won't have time to get ready for them."

VII

That first autumn with Sarita, Lang lived, as he himself put it, in a giddy daze. He felt as if, after twenty or so years, he were being given *carte blanche* to return to the life of a moody and precocious teenager. In September and October the future of his show was in the balance. The network wanted to slash production costs, and they also wanted to shift "The Blue Hour" from its usual Friday prime time slot to the oblivion of a Tuesday afternoon hole. The alternative, they threatened, was outright cancellation. Accordingly V.P. Minkkinen and his team managed the intricate and difficult negotiations, but Lang refused to be cajoled. When Minkkinen proposed that he turn up to the meetings Lang gave one lame excuse after another.

In another arena Lang was proving to be full of constructive energy. For ten years he had not devoted himself to exercise other than cycling and the occasional charity soccer match, but now he embarked on an ambitious training programme. He started going to Gold's gym up by Järnvägstorget Square, and when a university friend made an innocent call to invite him out for a pint at William K., this friend found himself a few minutes later roped into an agreement to play badminton with Lang every Thursday night at 10 p.m. out in Hagalund.

One Wednesday afternoon at the end of October V.P.

Minkkinen called and said that the drawn-out negotiations had finally paid off and that "The Blue Hour" would go on into the next season. The only compromise, Minkkinen said, was that the show had been bumped from Friday to Thursday evening.

"That's sounds wonderful," Lang said coldly, "And who exactly do you have in mind to host this shit?"

He hung up and went to the House of Bourbon to see Vekku, whom he hadn't seen since the summer.

"Well, well, who have we here?" Vekku said. "Haven't seen much of you lately. Did you ever find that chick you were after?"

"Yes, I found her," Lang said. "Though I suppose you should say she was the one who found me."

"And was she worth it?" Vekku asked.

"Every minute," Lang said.

Vekku held up a bottle of expensive Irish whiskey.

"Care to have a glass?"

"I can't," Lang said. "I have to go and see a film with someone."

"With her?"

"Unfortunately not."

Sarita brought Miro to meet him under the clock at Stockmann's as they had arranged. Then Lang and Miro went to buy tickets to an animated film showing in one of Forum's smaller screening rooms. They walked around downtown before it started. Miro begged Lang for an expensive bag of chewy fruit candies from a specialty shop called Candy Pix, and Chrisshansetä paid up because he wanted Miro to like him. The bag of candies was huge and noisy, and Miro's small jaws chewed frenetically. Halfway through the film the bag stopped rustling and Miro stopped chewing and a little while later the boy threw up undigested fruit candies and some quite digested macaroni and cheese in Lang's lap. Then Miro started to scream that everything was Lang's fault; Lang washed off the worst of the mess in the men's toilet and handed the janitor his card, then he and Miro hurriedly left the theatre.

That night Lang slept in Sarita's bed. Miro lay tucked into his corner of the apartment and Lang still had the sickly sweet-sour smell of vomit in his nostrils. Sarita slept. Lang looked at her; he could not get enough of her. He looked at her as if she were a sculpture, just as she had said that first night she sat on his sofa. She had kicked off the blankets. Her toes were long and the big toes were slightly crooked. Her calves were thin. Her hips were slender and her pubic hair a well-groomed patch in the middle. The deep pit of her navel rose and sank with her breath. Her breasts were low and round against her chest and her hair spread out over her pillow like a dark waterfall. Lang went out into the kitchen to get a glass of water. It struck him that they always stayed over in Sarita's apartment, that she hadn't been to his place since that night in July. It was in part due to Miro, of course, but it was also due to something else; the fact that Lang liked spending the night here. He liked hiding out in this apartment with its two rooms, like a lair where he was far away from the demands of the world, from Mikkinen and his constant relaying of budgets from his publishers and their questions about how far he had come with the new novel, from the tour managers and their suggestions for time-consuming and poorly paid gigs in the country side, from the neo-Nazis who sent him e-mail threats demanding that he ban socialists, homosexuals and Swedish-speaking Finns from his show.

Neither stress nor evil can reach me here, Lang thought as he stood there in the blackness of the autumn night drinking a glass of water.

But in December, Lang later recalled, the melancholy he had felt over the summer sometimes flared up. His new life, both the one he was living with Sarita, and the rest, took its toll. On Thursday nights, after he had played badminton with his old university friend, he couldn't now fall asleep until almost five in the morning. Sarita's embraces didn't help, nor the shudders and twitches he experienced when he was spurting his seed into her. The sex simply woke him up more, he felt the blood rushing through his veins and how the messenger substances in his brain were working overtime. He felt both a great hunger for life and a vague anxiety about the inevitable progression of time. He became chatty and wouldn't let Sarita sleep: time after time he would lean over her in the dark, shake her bony naked shoulder and whisper "Darling, are you sleeping?" This soon began to get on her nerves. The photographer she worked for was an early bird and wanted Sarita to be there at eight in the morning, and so already before Christmas Lang was confined to his own apartment on Thursday nights. He noted somewhat despondently that he had not had the slightest problem with sleeping after exercise when he was ten, fifteen years younger.

But there was something else too. From the beginning of their relationship he had been plagued by a feeling of shame about his own body and it was something Lang had never experienced before. In the changing room at Gold's gym he threw covert glances at the young men with their strong chests, well-muscled abdomens and confidently dangling sexual organs that had not yet produced any children. Then he looked straight down at himself and saw only half of his passive penis because a small but nonetheless undeniable beer belly hid the rest from view. This humiliation was completely subjective and experienced in stillness and secrecy, but it was repeated time and again and soon it started affecting him even when he slept with Sarita. He was both turned on and alarmed by her boldness and independence, and sometimes when his wintry-dry and already somewhat loose skin rubbed up against her tight, well-moisturized body he felt ugly and insecure, and much less adept at making love than she was. Some nights Sarita gave herself up to pleasure with a forceful abandon – *regal* was the word Lang used. She lay on her back with her arms carelessly spread, that is, not even touching Lang, with her eyes closed and Lang had the impression that he could have been anyone, that Sarita took her pleasure without caring who was there to help give it to her.

One Friday afternoon a few days before Christmas Lang and Sarita gave her friend Kirsi a lift to the airport. Kirsi was going to spend Christmas and New Year with her boyfriend Miguel in Madrid. Lang sat at the wheel of the Celica and listened to the two women joke about Miguel's beautifully sculpted stomach, his six-pack. They drove through a grey and rainy Kottby and the women's talk, as light and carefree as lemon butterflies on a day in July, started getting on his nerves. When they reached the Tusby dual carriageway he could no longer restrain himself. He pushed the accelerator to the floor until the powerful engine had forced the car to 130 kilometres per hour and then, as the exit to Åggelby flashed by, he turned his head and snarled: "You sound like a couple of airheads. Are you really so shallow?" Kirsi giggled from the back seat, but Sarita looked coldly at him and said, "What are you saying, Lang. Do you have a problem with the way we talk?"

"Yes," Lang said. "I do, in fact. You sound so . . . fake. Like bimbos."

Sarita didn't answer, just looked pointedly out of the window. It was raining and the grey-brown landscape was only broken up by the occasional low-price warehouse shop such as Etujättis and Giganttis. But later, when they were driving back to the city and were alone in the car, Sarita said to him with a cool and hollow voice:

"If you think you have the right to dictate the level of conversation I have with my friends you might as well start looking around for a new lover."

It was their first real fight and in a way it lasted for several days. When Lang and Sarita walked into the apartment on Helsingegatan, Miro immediately sprang up from his seat in front of the TV and jumped into Sarita's lap.

"Hi Chrisshan," he said, giving Lang a quick look.

"Hi Miro," Lang said and went into the kitchen where he started preparing a bouillabaisse. When it was ready they sat down together to eat, Sarita and Lang sharing a bottle of dry Italian wine, all in complete silence. After they finished, Sarita put Miro to bed, and then she and Lang watched "The Blue Hour", also in silence.

Lang had chosen to wear purple that week: his shirt was a pale lilac shade, the tie somewhere in between white, pink and violet, and the jacket a deep purple. From his perspective as viewer, Lang was pleased with the ensemble, but Sarita didn't make any comment, about his clothes, or about anything else for that matter. The first guest on the show was Prime Minister Lipponen and then Siltala, the professor of psychohistory. Lipponen had been criticized all autumn for his disagreeable manner, and Lang had invited him and Siltala to debate the authoritarian inheritance in Finnish politics. Lang thought the conversation flowed well and had strong substance, but Sarita yawned a couple of times. After half an hour there was a commercial break and at that point Sarita said her first words since the afternoon: "Sometimes I get so sick of opinions I want to be turned into a sea anemone or something." Then she disappeared into the bedroom and closed the door. Lang shrugged his shoulders and turned off the TV. He took the bottle of wine and poured the dregs into his glass, then walked to the window and looked out at the dark, run-down courtyard. In an apartment across the yard from Lang, one floor down, someone was watching "The Blue Hour". The viewer was basically obscured – Lang only saw a pair of legs stretched out on a footstool – but the TV screen itself was clearly visible. Lang watched himself for a while. It was like looking at an old silent film, except in colour. He saw himself talking to a male film star who was notorious for his colourful life style. They were talking about what it was like to be constant fodder for the press. Suddenly there was a close-up of Lang and his face filled the screen. Since the sound, the words were absent he saw his own gestures and facial expressions with a fearful clarity. All of his tics and mannerisms were enlarged and exposed: he saw the exaggerated eagerness in his face, the expression closer to a grimace than anything else, how the corners of his mouth and his cheeks twitched when he was trying to speak emphatically. And above all he saw his hands, how they twirled and waved and flew in wide circles in front of him like two large clumsy birds and he remembered how V.P. Minkkinen was always bringing this up, that Lang had a somewhat too lively manner in front of the merciless lens of the camera and that he should learn above all to tame his hands.

Lang felt the distaste return, the feeling that had made him snarl and swear at V.P. Minkkinen and the studio director and everyone else all autumn. Who was he really, this purple-clad joker on the screen? And what did he have to say, what was the invaluable message he had which gave him the right to take up peoples' time on Friday evening when everyone was tired after five long, rainy days of work? Lang poured himself the last few drops of wine and left his place by the window. He walked with heavy, hesitant steps to the bedroom as if he already sensed the outcome: that Sarita would start talking to him the next day, but that she wouldn't caress his body, nor let him caress hers, until two full days had passed.

VIII

Rain continued to fall over the grey, water-logged city. It fell evenly and steadily, like the tears of gods resigned. In the days between Christmas and New Year's Eve Lang made a detailed plan for the spring season with V.P. Minkkinen and a research team: the work days were long and he spent many nights alone in his apartment on Skarpskyttegatan. The evening before New Year's Eve he returned to Helsingegatan, opened with his own key and found Sarita alone: she was sitting at the kitchen table eating yoghurt from a bowl.

"Where's the boy?" Lang asked immediately, because he had given Miro a Game Boy for Christmas even though Sarita had said he was too little and Miro had been extremely vocal in his appreciation of the gift and for the first time even of Uncle Chrisshan.

"He's with his dad for New Year's Eve," Sarita said calmly. "Or rather, with his grandmother. Marko's mother lives in Stensvik and that's where all three of them are."

Lang was confused and a little jealous. Miro had finally started accepting him as a welcome guest in the home – almost as a kind of father figure – so why did he have to leave now? To top it off Marko had spent Christmas elsewhere, in Turku or possibly Stockholm, Sarita thought, and Lang hadn't so much as thought about his absent rival for several weeks. Now his fear of the man whom he thought of as Sarita's ex-lover rather than as Miro's father was revived. Even though it had almost been four months, he thought, Marko was still a troubling, shadowy presence. Lang had not yet met him in person, he knew him only from the picture stuck into the frame of the mirror by Sarita's bed: a handsome, hard-edged face, his hair in a ponytail, the gaze penetrating and sharp. Lang was often the one who slept closer to the mirror table and so he sometimes rolled over in the morning and stared straight into Marko's hawk-like eyes. He had been meaning to ask Sarita if the photo of Marko, Miro and her could be moved somewhere, to a less conspicuous place, for example to a cupboard that could be locked. But he had never dared ask her and perhaps it was because of this cowardice that he now had an irresistible urge to question her and to protest.

"Are you quite sure that Marko is capable of taking care of the boy?" he said and then, "How is the mother anyway?"

Sarita looked at Lang with surprise and said, "Of course I'm sure. As long as Marko's stepfather was alive I would never have allowed it, but Jokke – the stepfather – died last summer. Kati, Miro's grandmother, is fine."

"What was wrong with Jokke?" Lang asked.

Sarita didn't answer for a few seconds, then said gravely, "He wasn't a good person."

Lang noted her seriousness and realized he should stop nagging her: his intuition told him this line of questioning would lead to a minefield. And yet he couldn't resist asking:

"And what guarantee do you have that *Marko* is a good person?"

"Marko may not be a good person, but he's nice to Miro," she said firmly, then said, "Why are you so interested in all this anyway?"

"Just that I'm sick and tired of this hide-and-seek," Lang said, "It's been going on since we met. Marko only comes here to pick up Miro when I'm gone. If I happen to be here, you and Miro take the tram downtown and meet Marko at a café and then you come home alone. Who is it you're ashamed of – me or Marko?"

Sarita shook her head with irritation and said, "I don't get you. This whole time you've talked about how our relationship has to be secret. I almost wasn't allowed to mention it to Kirsi and now you suddenly want me to introduce you to Marko! How do you want things to be?" She got up from the kitchen table, started washing out the bowl with the tap running, and said, "Anyway, it's not about my feelings."

"I see," Lang said, only partly satisfied. "And whose feelings . . .?"

"Marko's," Sarita interrupted. "He doesn't even know who you are. He only knows that there's someone, and without even knowing who you are, Marko is not exactly excited about your existence. You can't really think that's so strange."

There were thin but distinctive traces of the holiday tension left in both Lang and Sarita on the morning of New Year's Eve. They made love first thing in the morning in spite of this – Lang remembered this very clearly – they did it several times in a row, and Sarita lay back in the bed with her arms outstretched across its width. But she didn't say his name when she came, she didn't say "Chrisshan, ooooohhhh Chrisshan!" as she usually did when everything was fine between them. Afterwards she got up and went into the kitchen to get her cigarettes and ashtray, walking back into the room with nonchalance, naturalness and ease, as if they hadn't just made love to each other but been conducting a business meeting or some such thing and she just happened to be naked, and while Lang was looking at her with admiration and longing in his heart he wrapped the blanket more tightly around him and knew that he no longer could nor wanted to walk around naked in that way in front of others. It was something that belonged to youth, he thought, and he felt an echo of the strange embarrassment he had felt all autumn, feeling like a stranger in his own body, in the body that had given him and that was still giving him pleasure but which no longer looked exactly the way he wanted it to.

That afternoon Sarita went downtown to have a glass of champagne with her friends. Lang stayed in the empty apartment, but without really knowing why. He too could have arranged to meet someone, V.P. Minkkinen perhaps, or the friend he played badminton with, or me, but he didn't even try. Instead he put on some music. For Christmas he had given Sarita a box set of CDs with songs from the sixties and seventies, and told himself that it was to show her that more beautiful music had never been written before or after. Of course – and he admitted this to me much later – he had given her the box set so that she would understand the tones that had stuck in him when he was a child and which were replayed inside him over and over. He put on a CD that started with "A Whiter Shade of Pale" and continued with Lou Reed's "A Perfect Day". Then he walked over to the window and looked out over the courtyard. Rain. Wet, shiny asphalt. Brown and dirty-yellow walls, coldly-lit stairwells, most windows in the other apartments dark. But not in the apartment across from him and down one floor. There the same jean-clad, stretched-out legs and bare feet on the footstool that he had seen the night that he and Sarita had quarrelled. But now this mysterious inhabitant was not watching "The Blue Hour", rather he was watching a documentary presumably about Adolf Eichmann's trial in Jerusalem in 1961. At least most of the events took place in a courtroom and a man looking very like Eichmann often flashed up, invariably flanked by uniformed guards. The old songs playing, the steady rain outside and the black-and-white picture of Eichmann gave him a feeling of unreality. He recalled how he had stood at this same window before Christmas and seen himself as in a fun-house mirror; a mute and hollowly gesticulating media-clown in his purple suit. He realized that this image haunted him and that it suggested he had looked for life in all the wrong places, first in writing, in his novels, and in later years in the increasingly well-rehearsed meetings with made-up people – and their made-up opinions – under the hot studio lights. It struck him how much he had silenced within himself. Had he really run through two marriages and even his own son's transformation from gurgling bundle to gruff teenager? When had they ended, all those New Year's Eve celebrations with ritual fortune telling, Coca-Cola drinking children, staid dinner conversation, dancing to Springsteen and Abba songs together with other hollow-eyed and stressed-out parents. Where were they, all these friends of old, all with raised champagne glasses and their assured wishes for a new and happier year? For a few moments Lang felt sorry for himself and other lost and homeless people. But he also felt something like the tickle in his stomach he remembered from his teenage years at the thought of life's inscrutable greatness, and it struck him how remarkable it was that he found himself in the dusk-darkened apartment in a block on Helsingegatan where he shared the bed of a woman who said things like "sometimes I get so sick of opinions that I want to be transformed into a sea anemone or something" and who sometimes felt like a complete stranger to him. And then he thought about Miro who was celebrating New Year's Eve in an apartment in Stensvik with his mysterious father, Marko, and whose New Year's Eves were almost all in the future. And once Lang started thinking about Miro the image of his own son hit him with devastating force.

Johan.

Nineteen years, almost twenty. He had left for London almost immediately upon graduating from high school last year, when Lang had felt so stressed and worn-out that he hadn't even found the time to be there, not for the ceremony or the reception. Lang had only sent flowers and a short letter and about a week later he had deposited a large sum of money in Johan's bank account. And after that? A few brief e-mails to a hotmail account at the beginning of the autumn, letters that had remained unanswered, and nothing more after that. Lang could see in his mind Johan's lanky body, his thin arms and legs, his blond, always tousled hair. He took out his mobile, and rifled through his address book until he found the number that Anni, his first wife and Johan's mother, had sent him followed by a laconic "If you ever feel so inclined . . ." He hesitated for a long time with the phone in his hand, trying to tell himself that the phone was not charged enough for such an important call, that he couldn't cut the conversation short, summarily dismissing Johan after so many months. But the symbol in the right hand corner of the display showed four fully loaded lines and so Lang finally mustered the courage and pressed "Call". There were a number of rings and then a woman's voice answered, just as loud and clear as if she were answering from the apartment next door. Lang cleared his throat, then asked for his son. He pronounced the name in an English way, "Jo-han" as opposed to "Yo-hahn" and felt silly.

"I'm sorry, but Johnny ain't here, ain't been for a couple of days," the woman said; she sounded very young and Lang had the feeling that she was American.

"Do you have any idea where he is?" he said.

"I'm afraid not. I'm only staying here for a few weeks and I don't know that much about people's whereabouts." Lang wanted to ask: "staying where?" since he didn't know where Johan lived and the only thing Anni said was he shared a house with a few others, somewhere in the suburbs.

"Do you want me to give Johnny a message, if I see him before I leave?" the woman asked helpfully.

"Tell him his father called and wanted to wish him a Happy New Year," Lang said and noticed that he tried to make his voice light and neutral when he pronounced the word "father".

"Oh, so you're his father . . ." the girl said, and when she continued speaking Lang heard a new respect in her voice that had not been there before.

"I'm sorry I couldn't help you."

"That's alright," Lang said. "It's hardly your fault."

"If I see him, I'll be sure to tell him you called," the woman said, then asked politely, "How's the weather in Finland?"

"Greyish," Lang said. "Our winter stinks this year."

"Likewise," the woman said. "But have a Happy New Year anyway."

"Yes," Lang said. "And a Happy New Year to you too."

IX

When winter finally arrived a few days into the new year it came with more snow than Helsinki had seen for decades. The city was soon transformed into a fairy-tale land, smothered in white, ice-clear starry nights interspersed with warmer, overcast, still days when large snowflakes drifted down from a sky whose store seemed without end. By the middle of January there were enormous white banks of snow on the pavements, over which people created thin, winding, slippery paths. Sounds were muffled, Lang remembered afterwards, even the clamour of children on outdoor ice rinks and sledging hills, even the rumble of snow ploughs driving day and night, pressing great barriers of snow to the side of the roads so that the cars parked along the city streets looked like puffy cream pastries.

The sudden change in weather had a surprising effect on Sarita. When Lang wrote to me from prison to tell me about this particular winter and spring, he apologized for his vulgar language. He wished, he wrote, that he could have expressed the matter in a more delicate manner, but there really was no way around it: the snow had an aphrodisiac effect on Sarita. Simply put, it made her incredibly horny. And now, Lang said emphatically, there was no tension; now she held him time after time, whispering the words he thirsted to hear "Chrisshan, ooooohhhh, Chrisshan!" morning as well as night.

Lang quickly came to share Sarita's erotic preoccupations and the worries that had been plaguing him disappeared. Soon he was exclusively concerned with the business of living. During those winter nights he and Sarita wrote on each other's skin and drew pictures in each other's flesh, and sometimes Lang felt transported to a state of adolescence, ruled by the feverish will to life and the desire to spray one's seed onto the world entire. All this had a positive effect on "The Blue Hour", or "TBH", as people called it. All autumn Lang had seemed bent on professional self-destruction and his relationship with V.P. Minkkinen had been strained to breaking point. But now the Lang who had once been the incontestable leader of the Finnish talk show was resurrected. His lethargy and peevishness were gone, replaced by a daringness in his choice of themes and guests. His new-found energy was also evident on camera where he was on the ball and intellectually penetrating while remaining friendly enough to reassure his guests. Now, according to a pleased V.P. Minkkinen, the only sticking point was Lang's fashion sense.

One Friday when Lang had spent the previous night in his apartment on Skarpskyttegatan as usual, he came into Sarita's apartment a little after five in the afternoon. He placed two full shopping bags of food on the table and saw Miro sitting on the floor in front of the television.

"Hello, Miro," Lang said kindly.

"Hi," Miro said without looking up; he was absorbed by an animated film on MTV.

"Where is Sarita?" Lang said.

"She picked me up from day care, but then she had to go to the clothes shop and the post office," the boy answered in a monotone.

Lang started to unpack the grocery bags: broiled chicken, vegetables, spices, rice. Miro got up from his seat in front of the TV, tiptoed into the kitchen, stopped behind Lang and said,

"It was fun yesterday when Marko-daddy was here. We played on the Game Boy you gave me. We played 'Donkey Kong' and 'Tetris'."

Lang stiffened at this revelation, but he had become so trusting the past couple of weeks that he gathered himself almost immediately and thought there had to be an explanation.

"I see," he said calmly, "And what was Marko-daddy doing here?"

"He was here with me," Marko said simply, and Lang heard a deep love for his father in Miro's voice. Lang imagined two horns growing from his forehead; the tug of jealousy was so sharp he wanted to ask Miro, the six-year-old, if Marko-daddy had stayed the night. He only just managed to suppress the question and instead went back to preparing dinner. Miro stayed and watched for a while but then returned to the TV. After almost an hour Sarita came home, pulled off a pair of new black high-heeled winter boots and kissed Lang on the mouth. Lang nonchalantly set a dish-stand on the table, then came out with the steaming spicy Thai chicken. Once they had been sitting around the table for a while and Sarita had already had her first glass of wine, Lang said pleasantly but somehow addressing no-one in particular – the way you do when you say things you pretend are not important at all – "I hear that Marko-daddy was here last night." Sarita threw a quick glance at Miro and then one at Lang and saw through them both at once. She smiled at Lang in a way that made him almost lose his balance, then she leaned over and stroked his arm.

"He was here baby-sitting Miro for a few hours. Kirsi and I went to the cinema."

Lang helped himself to more chicken curry and looked coolly back at Sarita.

"What did you see?"

" 'The Road to Rukajärvi'," she said.

"Was it good?" Lang asked. Sarita smiled again and said, "Yes, it was good. And Marko left within five minutes of me coming in the door, in case you're wondering." She paused and then continued in a low voice, "I do love you just a little, Lang. Remember that."

When Lang wanted to describe how happy they had been that winter and spring, he often talked about the admiration he felt for the way that Sarita cared for Miro, as well as her seemingly boundless patience with Marko's unreliability. Lang also liked to talk about the silent agreement they quickly reached regarding household matters and the trivial arrangements of everyday life. He probably liked to tell me these things to convince me their relationship had not just been about sex, but there was no reason for me to doubt the validity of what he said.

Marko continued to avoid Lang, but when he returned from his unspecified trips overseas and sojourns in various Finnish cities, he always called and demanded to see his son, often without embarrassment and to help his cause, citing Miro's great love for him. Sarita listened patiently to Marko's explanations about why he had disappeared yet again. Frequently she would reorganize her plans – and by extension even Lang's – in order to accommodate Marko's wish to take Miro to the Borgbacken amusement park or to his mother's apartment in Stensvik for the weekend.

But that which impressed Lang the most wasn't Sarita's forbearance towards the invisible Marko, rather it was the daily interplay between her and Miro. Sarita could become thoroughly irritated by the boy. She could snap and swear at him, and at certain times, such as when she was wrestling to get him into his snow suit, she could even be a little too hard-handed. But Lang said she always knew where the line was drawn. She never violated Miro's integrity, never humiliated him, and if she had ever been a little too rough she swiftly apologized and hugged him with unmistakable love. And this meant that Miro loved her and trusted her to the point that he even had the occasional temper tantrum, something which only children of single parents, Lang insisted, do not always feel secure enough to allow themselves.

When Lang was observing Sarita and Miro's lives it sometimes happened that the flood gates to his own memory were opened and he retrieved small glimpses of a past that had been obscured in his memory for many years. He saw himself with Anni and Johan in a small apartment on Fjälldalsgatan in Tölö. It was the early '80s and they ate the same kind of quietly happy dinners that he and Sarita enjoyed now, and, just like Miro, Johan had liked to hide under the table and touch the grown-ups' legs. Sometimes Lang saw in his mind's eye the objects that had once been of crucial importance and that he since then almost never gave a single thought to: changing table, packets of nappies, wipes, an image of Johan who stopped crying once he was changed and dry and then lay panting and gurgling contentedly in the dark. He remembered the autumn when Johan had turned one but was still on the waiting list for day-care and Anni returned to her job at the radio station. Lang sat at home working on his first novel while Johan slept. When Johan woke up they went out for a walk. Day after day Lang pushed Johan's stroller through Hesperia Park in a seemingly never-ending rain shower. Johan sat upright in the stroller, wearing a turquoise hat that tied under his chin, smiling at passers-by. They stopped at a café and bought meat pastries for Lang and strawberry ice cream for them both. But once they were home and it was time to eat Johan spattered salmon- and potato puree onto the walls and Lang became furious and grabbed the boy out of his high chair and literally threw him down on the ground and Johan howled with despair.

For more than a year Lang was haunted by images from the past. These memories hurt, because they reminded him of the coldness of his own childhood home and his inadequacies as a young parent. But now, when his inner archives were releasing glimpses not only of sadness and fear, but also of the occasional happiness that is always there although we humans so easily forget it, he felt something approaching atonement. And he was grateful to Sarita for being there close to him, and because she helped him remember without the sadness or shame taking over just by being the way she was.

Sometimes Lang had moments of something he would later call clear-sightedness but which at the time he chalked up to his neurotic tendencies. There were moments when he thought he heard a sudden abruptness or insecurity in Sarita's laughter. She could sometimes laugh a moment too early or too late at something that he or Miro or Kirsi said and at these times there was almost a cutting edge to her laugh, as if she wanted to cry or bite something or both. Lang knew that Sarita sometimes fled into an overly energetic and hard lustiness in order to prevent herself from becoming sentimental and he experienced days when she armed herself with cynicism and sarcastic one-liners to the degree that the cynicism and sarcasm obscured everything else going on inside her. He sensed that Sarita was a person who had been forced to grow up too quickly, who had been made hard and brittle by the conflicting demands placed upon her by parents or friends or Marko or someone else; he still didn't dare ask her about it. Instead he simply waited for her bad mood to be at an end, until she came over and kissed him on the mouth and smiled in the way that made him lose his balance inside. Lang, who had thought he was immune to such smiles, forgot at those times the doubt and disconcerting observations, he felt only an intimacy with Sarita and a strong longing within himself to get even closer. Somewhere inside him he was close to making a decision. And when his mother called him – this was at the end of March – and told him that his sister Estelle had been admitted to the hospital again, he decided then and there that he was going to confide in Sarita. He was going to tell her about his childhood, about his home, his parents and about Estelle.

X

We were different from the beginning, Lang and I. We had different starting points and that meant our friendship was weak and unbalanced from the start. But the friendship is still one of the things we have truly shared. Another is this: writing, fastening words down on the page, searching for a way to describe that which cannot really be told. And a third is love for Estelle, and grief over her amputated life.

Lang has been teasing me about my lack of imagination and talent since we were children. Lang is a surprising person, one who does not tremble at the outer reaches of the human experience. I do. Lang attacks, seduces, takes the initiative. I do not.

When I am poised to launch into a story, I make myself blind and deaf to my environment. But Lang has never made any bones about the fact that he despises the psychological realism I stand for, and as a result I was only allowed to undertake this narrative after so many sarcastic directives and prohibitions that I felt tied from head to toe. But instead of sharing with you the ironic and mean-spirited comments that Lang wrote in his letters from prison, I will let you read the end of a review of my fourth novel, *Night above Kallhamra*. Kallhamra is the fictitious name I have given the suburb where I grew up. And the following words, signed C.L., were printed for all to see in a well-regarded literary journal almost exactly seven years ago, a few months after my book had come out:

"... *Konrad Wendell's new novel is admittedly ambitious and far-reaching and it is driven by a moral ethos. And perhaps this is the very crux of the problem: Wendell wants so very much to do something with his book, and the result is that there is too much of everything in here. He loves his protagonists and wants to facilitate reconciliation left and right and the whole novel is therefore characterized by a clamp-like sincerity underscored by the fact that his characters are inevitably clumsy and unfortunate in their interactions.*

"*Konrad Wendell has in book after book demonstrated the laudable aim of depicting our immediate history and the shifts in the* zeitgeist *that have typified the different generations in the second half of the twentieth century and he has the sociological and psychological perception needed for such a project. However, Wendell often settles for description rather than analysis, and since his world view has a few fatal flaws – among them an obsessive and antiquated class perspective as well as a belief that all aspects of an adult personality can be traced back to childhood – the seemingly far-reaching story comes to feel surprisingly narrow. And since Wendell this time more than ever is also victim to another of his flaws, an overuse of historical detail, the result is mostly tasty morsels for the self-deluded, supposedly self-critical bourgeoisie. Konrad Wendell in fact brings to mind these words of Mallarmé speaking of Zola and the other naturalists:* Ils font leurs devoirs; *they do their lessons.*"

I quote this at length only so that you will get a sense of how detailed the instructions that Lang gave me four years ago were: Not a word about the early years! No attempt at psychological explanations on the basis of my childhood!

But now I have reached that part of the story where I can't go on telling it without explicitly breaking with these express instructions. And it comes back to Estelle. She's the point I can't get around. I can't bring her into the story and pretend that the past never happened.

Our suburb is in northwestern Helsinki. Its name makes no difference. I've already depicted it in both novels and essays and I don't want this narrative to become my own. I grew up in one of the large rental apartment buildings on the hill, a couple of kilometres from the shore with its gracious homes and mansions. Both the elementary and secondary schools were down there by the shore and for many, long years I wandered down the kilometres of hill with my rucksack, the last five years with a worn leather briefcase I got from my father. To start with I didn't know anyone who lived down there. All of my friends lived like me in the rental apartments up on the hill.

My father's relatives have lived in Helsinki for generations but without making anything of it. My grandfather's father had a detective agency on Mikaelsgatan at the beginning of the century. My grandfather, however, was a drunkard who quickly consumed the embryo of a fortune his father left him. My father Rurik Wendell was a loud but harmless man who worked in a hardware store his whole life and was eventually promoted to manager. He loved my mother, whose name was Maiju and who had grown up in the countryside outside Björneborg. I was the youngest, with two older brothers and a sister. Both Rurik and Maiju are already dead and so is my oldest brother Kaj who died in a car accident when he was a university student. My sister Karina was a Finnish champion of judo in her youth, now she is the mother of four children and works at a bank. My brother Kim is first mate on a ship and the last I talked with him he was working on one of the ferries between Helsinki and Tallinn. We didn't have much as children, but my memories are still mostly happy. But even though Lang always claims the opposite I don't think I'm particularly nostalgic or sentimental with regard to family life. I've never been back to our home on the hill and I have only sporadic contact with my siblings.

I say all this so that you'll understand how unlikely the friendship between me and Lang was. Because we did become friends and that almost as soon as the Lang family had moved to a townhouse close to the old cadet school, a stone's throw from the beach. Maybe Lang needed a loyal supporter he could always outshine. We were only ten, but there was no question in our minds as to who was the more talented. Or else he was simply lonely. For although Lang was handsome and attracted girls from a young age, and even though he was good at sports and made friends that way, he was never especially popular. The first few years in the suburbs there was something shy about him as if he were holding back, and it was as a teenager that he went through a personality reversal, becoming somewhat arrogant and coldly superior in a way that held everyone at a distance.

The Lang home was elegant, but the apartment was not quite as big as you would have expected. I think now that the family probably did not have as much money as they tried to make it appear. Lang's father's name was Stig-Olof and he was a lawyer at a distinguished law firm that had an office downtown. At home he was strict and distant, preferring to stay in his study to smoke and read work-related papers. When he emerged from his study it was always to pick up the leash that hung on the wall in the entryway and then take a walk with the family dog, Bobby, an Airedale terrier. The real lynchpin of the family was the mother, Christel: she was a formidable Swedish-speaking Finnish lady, the kind who takes charge and fixes things and never doubts that her understanding of a matter is the objectively correct one. Estelle was two years older than Lang, she also had dark hair. There are girls who have braces and poor posture and limp hair and only bloom once they are on the verge of adulthood, but Estelle wasn't one of them. She was a devastating beauty by the time she was thirteen or fourteen, so beautiful that I blushed and couldn't breathe as soon as she walked into the room.

Life could be messy up in the rental apartment on the hill, but I was never jealous of the Lang family for their lifestyle. Admittedly there was a cooling breeze to life down there by the shore, and I will never forget what it felt like to drive around those lushly landscaped streets in the September evenings when the air was growing cooler and the world was turned red by the last rays of the sun. But life down there was not simply grand apartments and landscaped gardens with silver spruce and hawthorn hedges. There was also something else to it, something between people, something difficult to articulate but which I sensed even in the Lang family: a sense of being set apart, an unwillingness, and inability . . . I still can't describe it in words. I only know it made me shiver and I knew I didn't want it in my life.

The Lang family lasted five and a half years in suburbia, then they moved back to the city, to an apartment on Petersgatan. Lang and I were sixteen and were about to start at secondary school, and the evening before he moved we sat in his room for the last time and talked about the years that had gone by and swore to maintain our friendship. Lang's room was up under the gable and some time after midnight Estelle came staggering across the neighbour's garden. She was about to leave for Massachusetts as an exchange student and she had been to a party to say good bye to everyone. She was extremely drunk, perhaps even high on hashish or marijuana. In any event, when she reached the large spruce tree in the middle of the neighbour's garden she stopped and, without looking around, pulled her trousers down, squatted and peed. It was August and there was a full moon that night. She sat with her back to us and I thought I had never seen anything more beautiful than her pale backside. When I managed to tear my gaze away and looked to my side I saw that Lang was also staring intensely at her, but his expression wavered between tenderness and despair.

When Lang moved back to the city he quickly gained new acquaintances. He was still not much loved or even liked, but now it was apparent that he had a degree of charisma out of the ordinary. Sometimes the group around him looked more like courtiers than teenage boys. And our continued friendship depended on me taking the tram or the bus into the city, because Lang never once visited the suburbs after he had moved away.

Late the following summer the beautiful Estelle came back from America. I took part in the welcome-home celebrations out on the Lang family's island in Porkala, but I didn't really see a change in her then, perhaps that she had started to smoke more. But she became ill that autumn for the first time. I visited Lang often and I remember the developments very clearly. First there were the surprising comments, often in the form of crude sexual allusions in the middle of what had been an ordinary, everyday conversation. Later on that autumn Estelle was like a caged animal. She could wash her hair and put on make-up and her best jeans and top, in preparation for going out, but an hour later she was back in the shower, washing herself, looking for new clothes and mumbling in an ominous way while she was doing so, or so it seemed to me and Lang. But she never made it out of the door and when I left and looked up at their apartment from the street she sat in the window smoking, looking right through me. She stopped going to school and spent the days drifting around on the street instead. She frittered her money away on video games in bars and attracted attention from soiled, shifty-looking men.

Christel tried in her usual energetic way to resuscitate her daughter. She attended frequent crisis meetings with Estelle's teacher and tried to reignite her daughter's interest in figure skating and the violin. But Estelle only became more and more apathetic. She stopped taking care of herself, she smelled of sweat, her hair was a mess and she had dirt under the nails of both her fingers and toes. All of January she lay motionless on her bed and only got up to sit and push the food around her plate at the dinner table or to sit in the window and smoke. Lang and I were already scared of her. And then one day she was suddenly gone, and the only thing Lang said was: "They admitted her."

I've never had the impression that there was any one thing that brought on Estelle's illness. If anything happened that year in the States – if she did too many drugs or was raped or any such thing – she never told anyone about it, not me or Lang or any of her therapists. And I can't say there's anything really wrong with her family, even though Christel and Stig-Olof's limitations became quite apparent that winter when Estelle went on getting worse and worse. Christel reacted in the way I mentioned, with a frenetic and insensitive over-activity, while Stig-Olof retreated completely. He couldn't stand to see his beautiful daughter so changed, becoming unkempt and ugly, and nor did he manage to stand up to his wife, even though he must have realized that her efforts only made things worse. In the apartment on Petersgatan, Stig-Olof had his desk in a small room next to the living room, closed off with only a thin glass door, and one could see him in there in his white shirt with the sleeves rolled up, sheltered behind a thick pile of court documents and with his pipe smoking in the ashtray. One ice-cold day in January – it was a few days before Estelle was taken away – I saw Lang go in to his father and I heard him say that he had to do something, that it was his duty as a father to tell Christel to leave Estelle alone and see to it that Estelle receive the care she needed. I stood in their front hall; I was pulling on my coat and was about to leave, and I saw Stig-Olof's eyes look first infinitely tired, and thereafter empty and dismissive, and then I saw him get up from his chair and walk over to the window where he stood and looked out on the icy and snow-covered Petersgatan and, with his back to the room and with a very small voice, he said to Lang: "I don't know what to do."

Most of what I have just told you and more, was what Lang intended to tell Sarita during the clear but blustery spring days when they went to see Estelle and then holed up in a hotel in a little town about halfway up the country.

XI

It is a chilly morning in the middle of April. Lang and Sarita toss a suitcase into the boot of the Celica and set off on their journey to the north. A few weeks earlier, a mild and fine Saturday night, Lang received a telephone call. He answered and heard a still forceful voice say, "Hello, it's your mother. Unfortunately Estelle is sick again." Lang stood there with the mobile in his hand. He looked out of the window and saw the unknown television watcher with his outstretched legs and bare feet at his post across the courtyard, and he looked up and made a note of the light and shimmering evening sky. After a while Sarita asked him what was wrong. Lang did not answer at first, but later that evening he told her that his sister was sick and that he hadn't seen her for years.

"Why haven't you told me any of this before?" she said, and then Lang told her more of Estelle and the history of her illness.

There wasn't the slightest hesitation on Sarita's part. "We're going to see her," she said. "We'll take a few days' holiday and go and see her. And then we'll have a romantic mini-holiday together in a small town where there's still snow on the ground. I'll check with Kirsi to see if she can take Miro. And if she can't, then Marko's mom probably can."

Before they drive away Lang makes sure the Celica is well-supplied with CDs. The Celica is a divorce car, a consolation purchase that Lang acquired when he began to sense where his second attempt at marital bliss was heading, and it has a ten disc changer that can be programmed to play in a particular order.

While they drive Lang tells Sarita about his family. He plays "Kind of Blue" and says that Stig-Olof has a fondness for Miles Davis. Then he plays Bowie's "Pin-ups" and "Aladdin Sane" and says that "Sorrow" and "Lady Grinning Soul" were Estelle's favourites. Because suddenly he wants Sarita to know, he wants her to understand who Estelle had once been and why the Estelle they are on their way to meet is completely different.

"Was Estelle beautiful?" Sarita asks. "Was she 'the prettiest star'?"

"Yes, she was beautiful," Lang says. "But she isn't any more."

Then they drive through Tavastkyro and into southern Österbotten and Lang plays his music and taps his fingers on the steering wheel and sometimes he sings along to the refrain, but he has stopped talking. They have coffee at a petrol station in Koskenkorva and when they get back into the car Sarita says:

"Do you have anything that was recorded later than, say, 1990?"

"Like what?" Lang says, surprised.

"Anything," Sarita says. "Manu Chao, for example. Or Alanis or Ultra Bra or Björk. It can be cool or angry or whatever, as long as it's not too sad."

In the evening, around eight o'clock, they arrive at the town where they are going to stay. Lang has booked a room at the main hotel, Stadshotellet. He sees the young woman at the counter give a start when she recognizes him and he can see she wants to say something, probably about "TBH", but she resists the impulse and continues on in her cool and professional manner, as if Lang and Sarita are just a regular pair of lovers in for the weekend. When they are finished unpacking they have dinner in the hotel restaurant where they are served old-fashioned food: lobster bisque, poached pikeperch with shrimp sauce for Lang, chopped steak and onions for Sarita. They are the only guests and Lang hardly touches his food, he isn't feeling well, he says, he doesn't know why, but he isn't feeling well. That night he is still upset, but he wants to make love, he says that if only Sarita caresses him and he her he will start to feel better. Later, shortly before falling asleep, when they are entwined in each other's arms and Sarita's head is resting on his shoulder and she plays with the hairs on his chest she says:

"Do you know that you don't have a smell? You are The Man without a Scent, wouldn't that make a great title for a book? You should write a novel with that title, Lang, it would be a best-seller."

And Lang answers sleepily, "I don't know if I'm going to write another book. And I don't know if I want to continue with 'TBH' either. I want to live."

Lang and Sarita ate an early breakfast, then drove to the hospital. It was more than a hundred kilometres further on and they drove through several more towns with their own quaint hotels. Lang was the one who had wanted to stay that far away; if they stayed too close to Estelle he would not have been able to keep her from his thoughts during the days they were spending on their own, he told Sarita. They drove through a bare but slowly burgeoning spring landscape; snow still lay on the ground here and there, in rapidly melting pockets. A gusty wind rocked the car on the long straights, and up there, in the icy blue yonder, the fair weather clouds swept by restlessly like big white ships.

They turned down a wet and muddy gravel road that led to the hospital which was set in beautiful parkland. Tall pine trees and a few winter-bare oaks surrounded the main building. At the information desk in the main building they talked to a friendly young woman who instructed them to go to the annexe, a low, practical modern house in white brick, and there, in a ward corridor, they found Estelle.

She was walking to and fro, mumbling in a low voice, and she was wearing a coat and hat even though she was indoors. She and Lang caught sight of each other at the same time. They both stopped and looked at each other shyly. Estelle was the one who broke the dead-lock.

"Hi, Christian," she said without expression. "I've been waiting for you."

Lang hesitated for a second, then walked up and hugged her. Later he would say that it was as if Estelle had crumpled up and shrunk since he had last seen her. She had also put on weight and somehow lost definition at the edges from all the medication, and later on – when I called and asked if he thought I should go to see her – Lang said to me: "I don't think so, Konni. I don't think you could take it."

When Sarita said hello to Estelle she stretched out her hand and said Sar-*ii*-ta with a Swedish pronunciation, instead of the clipped S*a*-ri-ta she normally used in Finnish. The rest of the afternoon she spoke Swedish with both Lang and Estelle, and Lang noted that her secondary-school Swedish was very good. But at first neither Sarita nor anyone else said anything. They walked around the park, on a well-kept but still frozen gravel path, and not one of them spoke. Then Sarita broke the silence. She looked up and said, "The sky is so blue today it almost hurts my eyes."

Estelle looked at her with eyes as dark as coal in her pale face and she said, "Blue is the colour of psychosis, did you know that?"

Sarita didn't answer, she simply tucked Estelle's arm under her own and they walked like that for a while. Lang followed behind until Sarita turned around and pulled on his sleeve to indicate that they should walk in a row.

"You know, Chrisshan," Sarita said. "Now that I see you and Estelle together I can see the resemblance."

Estelle gave a short, sharp laugh, and said, "Once upon a time we looked like each other. But now I'm so ugly."

"Don't say that, Essie," Lang said vehemently, "you're not ugly at all."

Estelle looked him in the eye and said in a tuneless voice, "She mispronounces your name, Christian, you do hear that, don't you?"

"So what?" Lang snapped, and then went on with an intensity that even startled himself. "I love hearing her say my name in that way. I love everything about her." Sarita pressed his hand and then started to run, pulling Estelle with her. They ran out on to the muddy, yellow-grey lawn and she had Estelle's hand in hers and Estelle followed without protest even though she moved with an ungainly and waddling gait, like a wounded bird.

When they had finished lunch in the cafeteria in the main building they took a tour of the annexe. Then they went to Estelle's room which she shared with a young woman who was home on a leave of absence. Estelle sat down on her bed and belched. Lang went to the window and looked out at the beautiful park. Sarita pulled off her woollen jumper, walked up to the small mirror hanging on the wall and started brushing her hair with a brush she had picked up from Estelle's bedside table. Sarita wearing a sleeveless, almost ankle-length black dress with large black work boots.

"You have beautiful armpits, Sarita," Estelle said from her perch on the bed.

"Thank you, Estelle," Sarita said peaceably. "Can you lend me some hair pins?"

Estelle nodded.

Sarita walked across the room, picked up a few pins from the nightstand and then went back to the mirror.

"In American television you aren't allowed to show nude armpits," Estelle said. "Especially not if they're unshaven."

"Why not?" Sarita said.

"I don't know," Estelle said. "Probably because they remind Americans of the existence of the adult cunt."

Lang turned away from the park that was bathed in the sharp spring sunlight. "Essie . . . please . . ." he started, but Sarita made a reassuring gesture and he stopped.

"Of course, yours are shaven," Estelle continued in the same matter-of-fact tone. Sarita didn't reply at once. She left the mirror – her hair was now piled in an untidy knot on top of her head – and went to the bed and took Estelle's hand and said: "Come on, Essie! I saw a shelf with games in the community room. Couldn't we play something all three of us?"

Then they played Scrabble all afternoon, though in Finnish. Sometimes Estelle mumbled impatiently while she was waiting for her turn and sometimes she made rude words, but more often she built words that Lang firmly said did not exist, such as *oudokki*, which could mean "strange person" but which was actually a word Estelle had made up. At first Lang was quiet and ill at ease, but Sarita simply laughed and applauded Estelle's numerous inventions and her eyes seemed to say to Lang "Why not?" And slowly, slowly Lang warmed up and joined in. And when he finally laughed, Estelle looked at him with her black eyes and then she too gave a small smile, a little askew, stiffly, as if she couldn't quite remember any more how it was done.

XII

It was already ten o'clock when Lang and Sarita finally got back to their hotel. They decided to order room service and had food and wine brought up. Once their dinner arrived they lay on the bed, half-clothed and ate their warm sandwiches and drank wine straight from the bottle and talked, but only about everyday matters like moles, different kinds of cats, and people's tendency to do things at the last minute. When they had finished their hunter's sandwiches and put the plates on the floor, Sarita said languorously, "Come over here, Lang. I'm in the mood for love."

But Lang rolled over on his back and stared up at the ceiling.

"Not yet," he said. "I don't feel like it."

"What is it?" she asked, coaxing his shirt tails out of his trousers, then caressing his stomach.

"Please," he said quietly and lifted her hand away. He raised himself up on one elbow and kissed her on the neck.

"I don't know what it is," he added, "I feel both happy and sad. I can't explain it any better than that."

"Try," Sarita exhorted. Lang was silent; the thoughts tumbled around in his head. Sarita, who had been sitting up in bed, snuggled down close to him and put her arm around his middle.

"I think I'm a little angry with you," Lang said.

"Why?" Sarita said and sounded genuinely surprised.

"Because you said that Estelle and I look alike."

Sarita waited a while before replying. She lay motionless and kept her arm around him. "Don't censure me," she said in a low voice. "I've had enough of that."

Lang at once felt badly. He stroked her hair and said, "I didn't really mean it. I'm just jealous of you. Jealous and full of admiration." He paused, then added, "I don't understand how you could get along with Essie so well. You had no trouble connecting with her."

"There's nothing remarkable about that," Sarita said. "I felt as if I understood her. People who act super-normal are much more difficult to work out."

Lang laughed a short, mirthless laugh, and said in a tone that was even more bitter than he had expected, "There's nothing I've spent as much time on as trying to appear normal."

"You are not Estelle," Sarita said. She emphasized each word. Then she continued, "But you were close when you were younger, isn't that true?"

Lang didn't answer. Sarita said: "She loves and worships you, but she also hates you. You are like the sun and the moon, you two. Every star has its black hole."

"Cut it out!" Lang said irritably. "Are you going to get the tarot cards out too?"

"Your stomach muscles are so tense," Sarita went on unruffled. "I think they've been this way all day."

"And why do you think that is?" Lang asked, already somewhat appeased.

"Because you have been trying to prevent her pain from entering your body," Sarita said. "Some people do that. They seem to be able to stand almost anything, but they do it in a distant, overly rational manner. They have a strong sense of duty and withstand crises like tense, hard bundles."

"Shut up!" Lang said in a muffled voice and fought hard to keep the tears back. Sarita had put her hand under his shirt again and he felt her cool, soft fingers glide along his stomach towards his chest. And at last he felt the release. His body started to relax and the question was simply which was going to come first: tears or lust. It would be the latter.

They spent two days and three nights in the little town. It was as sunny on Saturday as it had been on Friday, but also as windy and cold. Lang and Sarita stayed in bed almost all day. They lived on cold coffee and mineral water and the croissants that they ordered through room service. Sarita still had the habit of drifting off as soon as they had finished making love; she somehow extracted herself from the whole situation, Lang said, sometimes she lay on her back and moved her legs in the air with a circling motion as if riding a bicycle. Sometimes she sat up abruptly and started checking her calves and knees to see if she needed to wax them or not. Mostly she simply stood up and started walking around the room naked in the way that had made Lang insecure and shy all winter. But now he was no longer shy; he was drunk with love and desire and walked around the bare, impersonal hotel room just as naked and as easily as she.

Several times that day they had been meaning to walk along the narrow river that flowed through the town. But each time they had showered and brushed their hair and watched the news on TV one of them would happen to touch the other, or else their eyes met, and they would start kissing, and half an hour later their bodies were warm and sweaty again. Only after dusk did they manage to get outside. They had dinner in the only Chinese restaurant and ignored the whispers and subtle glances in their direction from the neighbouring tables, and then they walked down to the river and saw a comedy with Tom

Hanks and Meg Ryan at a cinema called the Grand even though it was very small.

On Sunday morning it started to snow. And it was this day in particular, their second, and the last outside place and time, that Lang would later remember; he would always remember the day that Sarita cracked the door to her past life, and he had listened.

By noon on that day the whole town was covered with a thin layer of powder. Lang felt deliciously spent and he suggested that they finally attempt that walk along the river they had been planning. Sarita who was standing by the window looking out at the snow had nodded absently. Then she walked through the room without a word and started to put on her knee-length red leather coat.

They followed the river out of town saying nothing. The yellow and brown three-storeyed buildings typical of the old centre gave way to wooden and brick single-family homes that had their own attached gardens. Then these houses too stopped and the river and the road that followed it continued on into a wide open whiteness, through snow-covered fields without a single person in sight, and where the monotony of the landscape was broken only occasionally by farms and from time to time a barn.

"I grew up in places like this," Sarita said at last. "Pieksämäki, Riihimäki, Parkano . . . People think it's romantic to have a father who worked on the railway. They imagine whistling steam engines and tender goodbyes at the station, the kind of stuff you see in black-and-white films." She stopped and Lang said:

"It doesn't sound as if you'd like to go back."

"There was nothing the matter with any of those places," Sarita said. "But there's nothing romantic about starting a new school every two or three years. It was hell. Should we turn back?"

Lang nodded and they started walking. It was snowing more heavily and the cluster of trees that signalled the start of the houses looked like a blurry dark shadow about a kilometre away. They walked about a hundred metres without saying anything, then Lang noticed out of the corner of his eye that Sarita was looking at him.

"I want to tell you about me and Marko, Lang," she said. "Is that OK?"

"Of course it is," Lang said lightly. "You know you don't need to ask."

"I know no such thing," Sarita said. "You always get unbelievably nervous whenever Miro or I so much as mention his name."

"I do not," Lang said stiffly. "That was only in the beginning."

"When we moved to Helsinki . . ." Sarita began, while she trudged on, the snow blowing into her face. She then proceeded to tell him in detail the story of her life, a story that Lang had already pieced together from snippets. How her mother had been forced to take two jobs to cover the cost of living in the capital. How her father had started seeing another woman; how the family had turned into three strangers who sometimes bumped into one another in the evenings and how she, Sarita, had been treated as an outcast by the others in her class at the suburban high school she attended. How she had started hanging out at cafés and bars downtown and falling into bad company, how she had tried drugs and started sleeping around. And how Marko had come into her life like a knight in shining armour. Marko, who was a year older and had problems with his stepfather Jokke, and who drifted through life without a steady job or a place to stay.

"When I met Marko I was eighteen and on my way to being expelled from school," Sarita said and put her arm through Lang's. "But Marko got me back on track. He had left school himself without graduating and he told me he didn't want to see me make the same mistake. There was . . . It's hard to explain, but when I met Marko it was like meeting my twin – a twin who made me incredibly horny." Lang heard the intensity and eagerness in her voice, and felt the usual stab of jealousy when she mentioned Marko's name. He wanted to drop her arm in order to show his vulnerability, but didn't. Instead he went on listening attentively.

"I had been so alone," she continued. "And Marko and I grew close very quickly. My father had moved away and Marko lived with me and my mother that first autumn, until my mother met Heikki. Then Marko didn't want to stay there any more. He was afraid that Heikki would start to drink and become violent like Jokke."

Lang and Sarita had reached the trees by now, and the first houses and side streets. While they walked through the town Sarita told him about the winter she had been preparing for her high-school exams, how she had studied during the day at the local library, how Marko had found a job in a video shop and started working out regularly and been far less restless than before. About how she met him downtown every day and waited for him to get off work and how they then wandered around a wintry and empty Helsinki, often long into the night. And when she talked about this she looked over at Lang quickly and said, "And then we slept with each other in the snow, often in some park." At first Lang didn't understand what she was saying, it took a long time for the words to sink in. But when he caught on, he unhooked his arm from hers, turned to her and said,

"You did what? You did it outside in the middle of winter? In the middle of Helsinki?"

Sarita shrugged and said, "What else could we do? Marko didn't want to come over to our place any more since he was afraid of Heikki. And we couldn't go over to Kati and Jokke's either."

Lang felt his cheeks start to heat up and his heart started thumping with jealousy and excitement.

"But how . . .," he began. "I mean, where did you do it? Wasn't it *freezing?*"

"I don't remember where it was," Sarita said evasively, "it was so many years ago."

"Bullshit," Lang said dryly. "Your life is too short. There's no 'so many years ago' for you yet. Just tell me."

His gaze met Sarita's and he saw both anxiety and desire in her eyes. But her voice was neutral, almost bored as she recounted, "Once we did it behind Sörnäs metro station. I remember that place because I came down with a high fever afterwards. Another time we did it in a playground in Skatudden, close to the ice breakers."

They walked together in silence. Lang looked into the black water of the river and tried to digest what Sarita had told him.

"Please don't be jealous, Chrisshan," Sarita said after a while. "Haven't you ever been bewitched by someone?"

Yes, by you! By you! Lang wanted to shout, but he didn't.

"I don't know," he mumbled. "Maybe by Anni, my first wife. But we never shagged in a playground, that much I know." He paused a few seconds, then added, "So Miro was conceived in snow and ice?"

Sarita didn't answer, she just smiled sadly and leaned against him and said, "Will you put your arm round me for a while?"

Lang wrapped his arm around her. She felt small and bony under her thin leather coat.

"If you were so crazy about each other, why the hell did it end?" he couldn't help asking.

"I was only nineteen when Miro was born," she said. "Marko was twenty. We tried, but . . ." She fell silent, then continued, "Marko was too restless. And he had bad friends. He was in the army when Miro was born, and he liked it. Once he was back in the civilian world he was calm for a few months, and he was sweet with Miro. But then he started to disappear, first for a few days at a time, then for weeks on end." Sarita was looking down at the ground now and Lang could see that the memories hurt her. Still she went on, "The day before Miro turned one Marko was arrested for breaking and entering and for possession of stolen goods. He got seven months, so I began to realize that I was going to have to take care of myself. When he came back out it was too late. I had started at the university and all I wanted to do was study and take care of Miro. And Marko, he was full of all these . . . ideas." They were almost back at the hotel.

"What kind of ideas?" Lang said.

"Marko was always reading a lot," Sarita said. "He reads both newspapers and books, but he interprets things in his own way. And he had met someone in jail, and he had new . . . political ideas. About cultures and religion and the like. As soon as we had separated he went over."

"What do you mean 'went over'?" Lang said. "I don't understand."

"Over there," Sarita said reluctantly. "To that place . . . To fight."

Lang stared at her. "To fight? Do you mean, to the Balkans? To Bosnia?"

"I think that was it," Sarita said. "Or else it was Croatia. It doesn't matter which. He came back almost immediately. They — whoever they were – didn't want him."

"For God's sake!" Lang said outraged, "Why would an ordinary Finnish man with a small child go to . . . I don't get it."

"I don't know," Sarita said. "He wanted to tell me about it, but I wouldn't listen. I just know it was a blow when they didn't want him. Marko thinks he's strong and invincible. He doesn't realize that he can come across as being tightly wound, a bit unstable."

"What about you," Lang said. "Do you think he's unstable?"

"Sometimes," Sarita said in a tired voice, "Can we talk about something else now? I've told you all I wanted to."

That night, their last at the hotel, Lang had already forgotten the part about how his beloved's ex-lover once tried to enlist in a mercenary army. Instead he was consumed by the thought of the adolescent Sarita and Marko in the snow, and when they got in bed he asked her to tell him about how she and Marko had lain together in the park in Sörnäs and the time they had done it next to the ice breakers. And Sarita did as he asked. She talked about the clouds drifting over the black winter sky, the warm yellow light from the windows of the nearby apartment buildings, and above all she talked about the sharp contrast of the biting cold beneath them and the heat and hunger and wetness inside and between them and she described how they kind of melted into each other, she and Marko, and became a single living source of heat in the coldness and death that otherwise reigned in the dark, blustery winter-city. And while she talked to him Lang lay pressing his body against hers and listened to her story and heard in her voice that she became turned on and warm from her memories and from talking and he both heard and saw that she had her hands under the covers and was slowly fondling herself and then, Lang told me much later, he was gripped by a wild, frenetic desire, more overpowering than he had felt before, that was, he said, almost unreasonable with regard to the fact that they had already been making love over and over for the past two days, and before he knew what he was doing he had ripped the sheets away and was on top of her and she accepted him without hesitation, and later he recalled that she lifted her legs to the ceiling, as wide as she was able and he heard her cry out "Come! Come!" and the remarkable thing, Lang said to me, was that in that very moment he did not feel like an impostor. He felt that he *existed* and that he *lived* and that he *filled* her and he never even thought about the possibility that maybe she lay beneath him and moaned and cried but was perhaps also looking out of the window at the snowflakes that fell over the little town and sparkled when they passed through the band of light from the street lamps.

XIII

I want to take you back to our teenage years before allowing this narrative to embark upon its inevitable conclusion. I don't know why I'm doing this, just that I have to and that Lang would mock me and say I'm wading up to my knees in affectation. He would say that the world I grew up in is a ghost-world, a distant illusion without a point of contact with the world we're in now, and therefore with no relevance to the people we have become. But I think Lang is mistaken, and that those thinkers are right who say that every person's fate has its roots in the time he or she comes from. And even though I know that he would vigorously protest and claim that I was projecting, that it's me and not him I'm talking about, I will suggest that Lang himself fell victim to this. For example, he misjudged the extent of the gulf between Sarita's basically inert and passive nature and his own drive constantly to measure up, to conquer. And more importantly he never saw the chasm that opened between his own desperation and Marko's. Lang's despair was rooted in his fear of aging and having his store of experiences declared worthless, and it is a fear that every adult Westerner carries today. But Marko's despair was rooted in something else, and it went deeper, was wilder and more absolute and therefore more dangerous. And I, who have known Lang since we were children, wonder if he could really have been as

86

blind to these signs as he appears. Perhaps he saw the danger all along, but wanted to continue anyway? And then this question presents itself: did Lang understand or sense the depth of his own darkness? Or did he understand it when it was too late, that night when he – shaking and as pale as a ghost – picked me up in his Celica from Tölö Square?

The island that belonged to Lang's family was in the outer archipelago, on the southern side of a wide and often windy and restless bay. The island was high, barricaded by cliffs and bluffs and generally inaccessible: it was playfully known among Lang's friends as Alcatraz. When we were in our later teenage years, Stig-Olof's health was already beginning to fail. He and Christel would spend a large part of the summer in town and Lang would invite friends out to the island. Sometimes there were big parties, half girls, half boys, sometimes it was just the inner circle of male friends who gathered to drink all night and swim and sail during the day. I had been out to Alcatraz every summer since I was eleven and I liked it out there even though it could be a forbidding place, the more so if the weather was bad. At that time, when we were in high school, I also felt close to Lang and I was totally unprepared for the idea that Alcatraz would be the site of the greatest humiliation of my adolescence.

It was the summer when Lang and I were seventeen and there were a few weeks left before Estelle was to return from America. Lang had already undergone the metamorphosis I mentioned: from having been successful but reserved to becoming arrogant and cocky in a slightly skewed, sometimes mean-spirited way. There were only a few of us out there that weekend, only the inner circle, as well as girlfriends of the boys who were in steady relationships. Neither Lang nor I were at that time. We drank heavily as always, but on the first day there was a good atmosphere. Saturday night Lang got the idea that we should drag the barbeque, food and alcohol to a small beach on the island's southern side, nestled between steep cliffs and rocks. There was a strong wind from the sea, the water had a green-shimmering, angry colour and although the sky was clear it was so cold that none of us wanted to swim. Instead we made a big fire and gathered around it. Perhaps it was the cold and the increasing despondency among the guests that triggered what was about to happen when the sun went down. Lang took up two stones from the shore and hit them together and when he had everyone's attention he started to speak: "As you all know my sister will be coming home in a few weeks, and you should all know that I'm not the only one waiting for her, there is someone who has been awaiting her arrival even more eagerly . . ."

What Lang went on to do was inexplicable to me at the time, and still is even today. He then launched into his piece with a rhetorical brio that increased the longer he went on and which anticipated his most inspired moments as host of "TBH". What he told everyone was about my secret, unrequited love of several years for his sister. He told this in great detail. I happened to be sitting a bit apart from the others and while I tried to look out over the ocean or into the fire and look completely indifferent he was touching on more and more pathetic aspects. When he got to the part where we one year earlier had watched Estelle's backside as she pissed on the grass, I yelled at him with a voice that I tried to make as manly, hoarse and threatening as possible: "Cut it out right now or I'll smash your face!" Lang looked over at me in a superior way. His eyes glinted in the firelight and he said, "You can always try, Konni. You can always try." Then he turned back to his audience and prepared to deliver the death blow.

A few months earlier, one Saturday in May, a few of us had been over at Lang's apartment on Petersgatan. Stig-Olof and

Christel had been away at Alcatraz for once and there were five or six of us boys sitting around downing booze. We became very drunk, the spring night was light and had an urgency about it and at some point Lang showed me a photograph album in which there were pictures of Estelle sunbathing topless. A little while later I took the album and sneaked out of the room – unnoticed I liked to imagine, though I saw the quick glance Lang gave me out of the corner of an eye – and locked myself in the bathroom. And if that wasn't bad enough, before I left the bathroom I took out one of the pictures of Estelle and I stuck it in the back pocket of my jeans. When I woke up the next morning at home in the suburbs with the picture of Estelle in my pocket my cheeks burned with shame, but by then the damage was done. And now, three months later, on an August night, Lang humiliated me in front of his friends. He told about how "Konni has been masturbating all summer to a picture of Estelle".

I was speechless and tried to keep the tears from running down my cheeks and was glad that at least it was dark out there. Some of the boys, Lang's most loyal followers who were prepared to lick his shoes clean if he stepped in dog shit, pointed at me and gave raw guffaws. But others were clearly uncomfortable and I heard one of the girls say to her boyfriend: "Can't he just stop? What does he think he's doing?" When Lang had finally finished I tried to catch his eye, and I did but there was no-one there. Or, that is to say, someone else was there behind his eyes at that moment.

I don't want to demonize Lang; I'm trying to capture his complexity. He apologized the very next day for what happened out at Alcatraz. He was pale and composed, but there was no mistaking his regret. When Estelle recovered after her first bout of illness, she and I became a couple. I loved her deeply and she and I were together for almost seven years. Lang never told her what I had done with the album and her picture and he never mentioned it even in a teasing way when we were alone. The last summer we were on Alcatraz Lang and his wife Anni and Estelle and I carved our names into the rock high above the beach where he had humiliated me. It was when Johan was a newborn, just before Stig-Olof and Christel sold the place. This was a time when Lang was decency incarnate; a young father in the middle of his university studies. A man who probably sensed the extent of his talent but had not yet been destroyed by it. He was supportive and helpful of my relationship with Estelle. He saw himself how happy she was during those days. She was calm and energetic and studied art history and sang in an a cappella group and not even her father's death caused her to lose balance. When Estelle left me a few years later I was convinced for a while that it was because she didn't think I was good enough to marry into her and Lang's family – such was the extent of the neurosis I had developed by growing up close to people like them, people who were more intelligent, attractive and worldly than I was. But when I suggested something along these lines to Lang about half a year after Estelle had become sick a second time, Lang looked at me with sadness and said, "How can you say that when you've been to visit her in the hospital and you see how she is? She knew she was getting sick again and she wanted to spare you the responsibility. Can't you see that?"

When Lang had read the first raw version of this story. I went to see him in prison. We argued, or rather, Lang was furious. He threw the manuscript into the air and let the pages float to the ground. He didn't sit, he walked around and around in the room and from time to time he yelled at me so much that the warders were ready to call an end to our meeting.

The part Lang hated the most was the part you just read,

which was the same in the original version as here. During our meeting in the prison he called my associations back to our youth a "desecration" and accused me of still being obsessed with Estelle. He asked me why I couldn't forgive him for something that happened one summer when we were only seventeen years old.

He was also displeased with a number of small things: he didn't like the direct quotes, and he found my description of events heavy-footed and awkward. Lang also thought I was too fixated with Marko from the beginning and that this focus diminished the freedom, warmth and desire that had characterized his and Sarita's first year together. "I asked you to write a story about love, not a story about a crime!" he yelled, and I answered, "I'm sorry, but in my mind they've become inseparable."

Lang and I are, as I have already noted, different. I admit to being guilty of always chasing words I think will recreate life in all of its lustre, in all its distinctive colours and shapes. Lang, who was talented, knew you always create a greater effect if you make your words evasive, just letting them brush against reality, suggest it.

I do not blame Lang for his anger. And yet I had set out to do my very best, to the extent that sometimes I felt it wasn't me writing, as though I were writing in words different from my own, and in a rhythm that was not mine.

I should come clean at this point: Lang broke off all contact with me. This is not an authorized narrative; it has no legitimacy at all.

XIIII

The next few weeks after the weekend away, Lang was – and these are his own words, banal by any standards, but especially from a member of the literary avant-garde – in seventh heaven. He daydreamed about how Sarita and he would move in together properly, and went so far with this as to make her accompany him to the showing of a large apartment in a newly-built luxury block by Merikantovägen in Tölö. But Sarita looked uncomfortable and shook her head and the whole thing ended with Lang having the kitchen and living room at Skarpskyttegatan renovated and painted. While the work was being done, he moved over to Sarita's and one day he said to her: "When Skarpskyttegatan is done we can renovate here too. See, patches have come off the ceiling and we can repaint and make the rooms look bigger . . ."

"Excuse me," Sarita said. "Aren't you forgetting something?"

"What?" Lang asked. He had already become used to her habit of suddenly pulling away and making herself distant. "Do you mean the fact that I don't own this apartment?"

"No, the fact that I don't own it," Sarita said dryly. "It's actually owned by one of Marko's friends."

"So call him and ask for permission," Lang said briskly. "He should be happy; it'll increase the value of his property."

"I can't afford it," Sarita said.

"That's OK," Lang said. "I'll pay."

"I can't afford it," Sarita repeated, and her voice was now as sharp as broken glass.

Lang and Sarita's first summer together was sunny and warm. Afterwards Lang would recall June and July as long, light months: dusty days with lazy conversations, trips to the Swimming Stadium and Borgbacken with Miro, endless nights with the salty and sandy smell of Sarita's sun-tanned skin and her encouraging love cries cutting through the white midnights.

There was the evening when Lang had arranged to meet Sarita and Miro in Sibelius Park. Lang arrived a little late and they were already there. Miro ran under the tall trees and played tag with another boy and Sarita sat on a green bench reading *Bridget Jones's Diary*. The sunlight sifted through the branches of the birch trees and then through her dark hair which had a bright red streak in front that summer. She had a light-coloured shirt with a broad collar, black trousers and expensive trainers from Union Five, and she was so lost in her book that she gave a violent start when Lang sneaked up beside her and kissed her on the cheek. After that she was in a bad mood all evening: when Lang teased her about sitting in the park with Bridget Jones instead of the novels by Ian McEwan, Joyce Carol Oates and Anja Snellman that waited next to her bed, she snarled that only hypocrites like him tried to convince the world that they were too good for a little entertainment now and then.

And then there was another evening, an evening when Lang had been gone almost a week and wanted to take Sarita out to an expensive restaurant in the city. At the tables next to them there were people in tailor-made suits and slinky dresses and among the suits was one of the most prominent Ministers in the Finnish government. Suddenly Sarita pushed away from the table, leaned back in her seat, pulled up her summer blouse and showed Lang a tiny, glittering silver navel ring she had acquired during his absence. Lang looked at the ring and Sarita's sun-tanned belly and out of the corner of his eye he saw that the Minister at the next door table was also staring at Sarita's bare stomach, his eyes wide with desire.

And then there was the night that Miro had gone to Sarita's mother and her new husband Heikki's summer place up in Virdois, and Sarita and Lang drank three bottles of wine in a bar down in the West harbour and spent the night in Lang's newly-renovated apartment. When they tumbled into bed Lang suddenly remembered that first night when they had talked for hours and Sarita had fallen asleep on his sofa and he had looked at her in the dawn light and wondered if he would ever get to touch her. Now she held his stiff dick in her hand and played with it as if it were her personal talisman, as if it were the most natural thing in the world. She laughed softly and Lang asked:

"What is it? What are you laughing at?"

"It's just so absurd," she said. "It's pulsating, it's so full of life, but very soon it won't exist."

"What do you mean *very soon?*" Lang asked, drunk but upset, and felt his erection fading. "I'm not that bloody old."

"I meant on the scale of eternity," Sarita said, but the harm was already done. Lang turned on his side and curled up so that Sarita had to let go of his penis, and then he muttered, "Spare me any further comparisons with the eternal. I can't stand it when you say things like that. I'm really starting to hate it!"

Sarita sat up in bed and leaned over to lick Lang's ear.

"You're actually more cat-like, Lang," she said. "Now that I think about it. I can't see you walking an Airedale terrier at all."

Lang was immediately soothed, turned over on his back and stroked her breasts and asked, "Is that a bad thing?"

Sarita didn't answer his question, just said, "Keep going. Don't stop."

"Is it a bad thing to be a cat-like man?" Lang repeated.

"No," Sarita said, already breathing more heavily. "It can be quite . . . attractive."

Lang looked at Sarita's silhouette above him in the dim light. He was overcome with a great, dizzying love of life and he felt a sudden need to get his thoughts off his chest.

"A man never knows where the line is drawn," he said and continued caressing her. "One moment he can be erotic, or cat-like or some such wonderful thing, and then in another he's gone over the edge and become a dirty old man. It's hard to dare to be who you are and it gets harder the older you get."

Sarita didn't answer immediately. She put her hand on his penis which was stirring back to life – already careless of its mortality – and then she said: "Silly, silly Lang. My silly, silly Lang."

At the end of July that year I left the cabin Gabi and I have in the Ekenäs Archipelago and drove in to Helsinki: I had a meeting with my publisher and I was also going to read the proofs for a German translation of an essay I had written about depictions of suburban life in contemporary Finnish literature. On the evening of my second day I ran into Lang and Sarita down by the Edesviken tennis courts. It was the only time I saw them together during the whole duration of their relationship. Lang had sunglasses with thin gold frames and his already greying hair was slicked back with gel – this was the disguise he used when he wanted to go unrecognized in Helsinki. He looked irritatingly well; tanned and fit. I couldn't help mentally comparing him to the wreck of a man who had come out to our cabin exactly two years ago; the hollow-eyed and overweight Lang who had chain-smoked black cigarillos and checked his watch every ten minutes and felt compelled to listen to the news summary on our old transistor radio every hour.

We had a couple of beers, and if I remember correctly it was a little place on the dusty Mechelingatan that had tables and chairs outside. Lang and I hadn't seen each other for more than a year and we talked about the usual, everyday things, about our current badminton game, and which of our colleagues had books coming out in the autumn, that sort of thing. Sarita didn't say very much, but she followed our conversation closely. In one of the letters he wrote to me from prison, Lang said – probably with a sneer – that later that evening he told Sarita about me, about our long friendship, my relationship with Estelle and described me as "a decent fellow and a good friend, but also a mediocre person who is inclined to envy those with genuine talent".

When we were already on our third and last round of beers, Sarita excused herself and walked into the restaurant in search of the ladies' room and then Lang couldn't keep from saying, "Isn't she . . .?" and giving a meaningful look in her direction. I nodded in agreement. Lang looked at me, suddenly earnest, and said: "I've always been impoverished when it comes to love. I used up what little store I had when I was young, with Anni and Johan. At least that's what I used to think before now." Then he smiled in a sad way and asked, "Are you up for a quotation?"

"Sure," I said. Lang and I had been challenging each other with obscure literary quotes since high school, and I, of course, usually lost.

"'I wouldn't want my youth back,'" Lang said slowly in English. "'Not with the fire in me now.'"

"Haven't the faintest," I said, also in English, after a couple of seconds of reflection.

"Beckett," Lang said smugly. "You should read the classics, Konni. You'll learn something."

The second Wednesday in August was unbearably hot. Lang was scheduled to tape the first instalment of the new season's "TBH" and then he was flying to Kuopio to play soccer in a celebrity match together with the bartender and ex-singer Vekku, the actor Suosalo, the writers Hotakainen and Raittila, the news anchor man Lind and many others. He had been going to stay in Kuopio until Sunday, at least that was the plan, but then, just before taping his show, when Lang ran down the stairs to the cafeteria in order to get a sandwich and something to drink, he sprained his foot. The taping of the show was delayed an hour, but after a doctor who was called in bandaged his foot and gave him some painkillers Lang was able to go through with the show almost according to the original format – only his monologue at the end had to be ditched.

As soon as he hurt his foot Lang called the people in charge of organizing the celebrity match to give them his regrets. Then he decided to surprise Sarita. Miro was still with his grandmother in Virdois and Lang imagined a romantic evening with candles, a delicious meal and a good bottle of red wine. When the taping was over he limped down to the garage, drove out of east Böle down towards Tölö and on into the city. He bought some food and wine at Stockmann's department store and then drove to Berghäll, parked his Celica by Åstorget Square and limped the two blocks to Sarita's apartment. As the lift was going up he started hearing the sounds of intense voices. Lang gave a pitying thought to the young couple on the fourth floor, the ones with the new baby and the infidelity and then he thought about how wonderful it was going to be to relax with his wine instead of running around on a soccer pitch. But when the lift passed the fourth floor it was quiet;

instead, the voices became even clearer as he continued upward. Still, it was only when Lang had stepped out of the lift and put his heavy shopping bags down in order to get his key out that he realized the sounds were coming from Sarita's apartment. When he realized this he froze. The sounds were pitilessly amplified by the naked surfaces of the empty stairwell. They echoed in his head, and life itself suddenly seemed to echo empty and hollow too, as if Lang had always been living at the bottom of a well but only understood it at this moment. He felt himself leave his body and become a sharp, naked consciousness completely motionless, listening to the remarkable mixture of cries. "Yes! YES!" Sarita panted, but in the next moment she moaned a half-pleading, half-commanding, "No! . . . No! . . . Stop! Not like that! NOT LIKE THAT!" while the man grunted, moaned and sometimes muttered short phrases whose meaning was not clear to Lang, focused as he was on Sarita's wild cries, rooted to the spot like a pillar of salt.

Suddenly Lang realized that he had an erection, that he was incredibly horny, and it was, he told me when he later described that evening to me, perhaps the most degrading part of it all, the fact that in the middle of this humiliation he actually found the sound of their voices and the muffled thuds against the wall and the squeak of Sarita's bed arousing. He couldn't help but distance himself from the situation as always and *analyse* it: he thought about the fact that maybe his and everyone else's eyes had become worn out, that they were so used to and so tired of all the flesh readily offered up to display, these last few decades, that the only thing left, the only thing that still genuinely teased and entranced was to *hear* others making love, without seeing them.

Lang finally woke up out of his daze, because the storm in there gave no signs of dying down. The muffled thuds came more rapidly and Sarita's perplexing mixture of delight and complaints had turned into a continuous babble, as if she were speaking in tongues and she was close to climaxing now, Lang could tell, and he was finally in a rage.

"What the fuck! Fucking hell!" he hissed between clenched teeth as he pulled out his key, forced it into the lock, turned it and pushed open the door that only went about ten centimetres before the chain on the inside caught it. The sudden resistance made Lang lose his grip on the key and the door slammed shut again with a loud bang. The apartment grew utterly quiet. It was as quiet on the stairwell. Lang became conscious of the warm sunlight flooding onto the stairs through the glass doors of the final landing. He heard the muffled sound of Helsinki traffic. He wondered why they had put the chain on the door since Miro was away and Sarita was sure that Lang had taken the afternoon flight to Kuopio. He clenched the key in his sweaty hand and opened the door again as far as he could and then shouted with fury and desperation in his voice, "What the hell are you doing, Sarita! Open up. OPEN UP!" He had no doubts about the identity of the man inside, he knew who it was, he had known it all along and now that he was faced with the truth all the repressed suspicions he had had during the past year came back to him. Not a sound came from the apartment. "Open up, for godssake Sarita, I want to talk to you!" Lang yelled like an abandoned child. "OPEN UP!"

After ten seconds a short-haired, well-built man of about medium height emerged from the inner recesses of the apartment. Lang recognized the face and the cold gaze even though his hair was different. Marko had a towel tucked around his hips and Lang noted that his erection still jutted out under the terry cloth.

"What do you want, Lang?" Marko asked threateningly. Lang looked at the strange, garland-shaped tattoos on his strong upper arms.

"I want to talk to Sarita," he said.

Marko leaned against the wall only a few centimetres from the door and crossed his arms over his chest. He gave Lang a disdainful look but said nothing. Lang heard soft sobs from the bedroom.

"Let me talk to her," he repeated. "Let me talk to her, dammit, I can hear that she's crying!"

"Don't be ridiculous, Lang," Marko said. "What's done is done. You were supposed to be in Kuopio. You have no business here tonight."

"Open the door!" Lang demanded. "Open the door, you motherfucker!"

"Do you really want me to open this door and let you in and then beat you so you can't appear on TV for several weeks?" Marko asked softly. "Is that what you want?"

They stared at each other through the opening in the doorway without saying anything. Lang felt fear grip him and looked away.

"Go on, Lang," Marko said and slammed the door shut. Lang heard his steps as he walked back into the apartment. He left the grocery bags with food and wine by the door, and walked out into the summer evening. On his way through the city he passed by tens of outdoor cafés with happy, noisy people. He passed hard drinkers as well as young, sweet-smelling people with smooth faces. He walked slowly and stiffly, as if he had aged a great deal. He dragged his foot without feeling the pain, he dragged himself through the entire city from Helsingegatan to Skarpskyttegatan, to the smell of fresh wood and paint that still lingered in the apartment.

XV

Lang retreated into his shell immediately after this discovery. After the initial period of mutually observed silence, Sarita tried to get in touch with him and when she realized that he was refusing to answer she simply tried harder. She wrote e-mails and sent text messages to his mobile. She left voice messages on his answering machine and she not only tried to reach him directly but also through the staff at "The Blue Hour" as well as at his publishers. But Lang ignored her and like a sleepy but methodical zombie erased all of her messages without listening to them. He was equally remote in his dealings with the rest of the world. A few weeks after the shock he went on his annual sailing trip with Uncle Harry and alarmed him with his lack of enthusiasm and his distance. The first evening, when they had anchored and settled into the lagoon with the broad low boulders, Lang declined both whisky and gin and sat silent while Uncle Harry studied the stars with his telescope. When Uncle Harry asked him about the state of his love life, Lang only smiled sadly and distantly and maintained his silence. And when Harry told him that he had spoken with Lang's mother and agreed that Estelle would live with Harry and his wife Marie when she was let out of the hospital, Lang didn't even react to this news which only a few weeks earlier he would have found both touching and reassuring.

He was not angry with Sarita for more than that first evening and the weekend, Lang wrote to me from prison. It was almost shocking how quickly the anger waned, he said. Instead he radiated a critical self-possession as if he had reached an important crossroads in life and was scrutinizing his past actions in order to reevaluate and renew himself. Those first weeks he was disturbed by the fact that he had been turned on as he stood there in the stairwell – "humiliated, mentally stripped, a brand-new cuckold" – listening to Marko and Sarita making love. He was tormented by the suspicion that there was something wrong with him sexually, that he had become, or perhaps always had been, perverted. He started to recall episodes from his past life when he had been alone but heard or seen other people in such a way as to excite his lust. He remembered the time he had been booked by mistake into an hourly hotel at a literature conference in Lisbon, and he remembered the effect the prostitutes' well-simulated sighs and moans and love talk in soft Portuguese had had on him as he lay on the other side of his thin wall. He remembered how as a very young man he had slept on the deck of a ferry to Sweden, in the sleeping section, and how in the early morning he had seen a teenage couple having sex on an upper bunk across the passageway. And he remembered how he had been working on his second novel in a borrowed apartment on Franzensgatan and how the woman who lived next door had masturbated for over an hour and how her pleasure-cries had sounded like one long mournful song and how it had been impossible for him to ignore it and keep writing. When Lang thought about all of these past events the memories sometimes made him so horny he had to take out his member and touch himself. And at times like these he sometimes thought, bitterly, how just a few weeks ago he had imagined that this average-sized and sometimes slow-starting member that he was now holding had made Sarita happy in a unique and singular way, despite the fact that there were billions of similar male organs in the world.

After a while Lang's shame changed its nature. Now it no longer centred on the body and its desires but included cursing his naivety and trying to find an explanation for what had happened. He asked himself why, despite his age and experience, he hadn't seen through Sarita's duplicity, even though the signs had been there all along, so clear they sometimes glowed: the mysterious, unwashed coffee cups, Miro's sometimes cryptic remarks, the foreign smell that sometimes turned up in Sarita's apartment, Marko's steady refusal to see Lang, Sarita's evasive and irritated answers when Lang had been away and he asked her how she had spent her time.

In another line of thought Lang imagined that all people wore a secret face under their everyday mask. This face was ancient, it was without name or individuality, it was EveryWoman and EveryMan. Each such face retained a trace of all people who had ever lived and were therefore bearers of atavistic behaviours and drives that were hardly functional in today's world, but that all people returned to, some more, some less. Even Sarita had such a face under the one that he had come to know and called "Sarita". Lang imagined that Marko had always been privy to this secret nameless face under "Sarita" while Lang had been denied access. And for some reason, Lang confessed, this thought which should have increased his jealousy actually offered him some *consolation*.

In the midst of this witches' brew of troubled thoughts, memories and explanatory constructions, Lang did what he had to do: he continued the new season, the seventh, of "The Blue Hour". But now everything went wrong. Lang was seemingly uninterested and indecisive during each programme's planning phase. He no longer prepared as meticulously for his interviews. He got on the wrong side of V.P. Minkkinen and the new studio director, a bearded TV veteran who had replaced Lang's former lover. Even Lang's screen presence, usually his strong suit, now seemed mechanical and uninspired, as if Lang didn't quite have the energy to listen to what his guests were saying. The downfall was swift and soon it became clear to everyone involved that they were witnessing the swansong of "The Blue Hour". It came as a shock to many since they had the magnificent successes of the winter and last spring season fresh in their minds.

When the downfall came, most of those in the know, among them even V.P. Minkkinen, blamed Lang's personal crisis. But in hindsight it is easy to see that the demise of "The Blue Hour" was not entirely due to the host's poor performance. At the end of the millennium the increasing infantilizing of the media world had taken a rapid turn for the worse. Country after country developed talk shows aping the puerile cheekiness of Jay Leno and Conan O'Brien. Network after network aired closet-fascist competitive shows like "Robinson" and "Survivor", as well as embarrassing voyeuristic programmes like "Big Brother" and the money-grubbing game shows "Who Wants To Be a Millionaire?" and "Greed". But soon the TV executives must have realized that even this was not enough in the battle for advertisers and viewers. An even purer form of childishness was needed in order to recruit some thirty or sixty minutes' worth of viewer loyalty from restless, sofa-based channel surfing. It was time for programmes such as "Guinness World Records" and "Impossible Task", "Jackass" and "Far out", and by extension the totally adult-free youth networks Moon and ATV. Thanks to this massive development the ideal age for a TV star rapidly dwindled to twenty-one and the magazines and programme guides threw themselves hungrily over all the new and fresh media profiles:

column after column was devoted to them, quoting their gems of life-wisdom such as "Life's a rat race, and I wanna be the Number One rat" and "I'm *so* into shaved pussies". As a consequence, Lang and "The Blue Hour"'s unsplashy intellectual profile started to look hopelessly old-fashioned and this was soon reflected in tumbling ratings and diminishing media attention: no-one was interested any more in making or taking part in retouched media portraits of the TV celebrity and novelist Christian Lang.

When V.P. Minkkinen received the ratings for September he became very nervous. He knew that the same numbers went to the bosses who in turn were connected to the reserved network owner Meriö, a fifty-five year old who had lived as a free-wheeling hippie at the end of the sixties but who had then turned to making money and who had risen to a media giant with a finger in every pie. Minkkinen knew that influential voices had long been advocating shutting down "TBH" and therefore he invited Lang to a strategy meeting, just the two of them. They met in the production company's offices six floors above the studio, in east Böle, and Mikkinen began by asking, "Do you know what our biggest mistake has been?"

"No, do tell me," Lang yawned and then stared dully out of the window. It was ten o'clock in the morning and he had been at Tapasta the night before, then gone to Soda and 10th Floor and ended up at Manala around four o'clock in the morning.

"That we didn't make you into the product from the beginning," Minkkinen said. "We should have named the show after you."

Lang yawned again, but didn't say anything. He ran his fingers through his hair and looked with interest at the fish in Mikkinen's aquarium.

"Kride, you have to get a grip on yourself!" Minkkinen said

sharply and rapped his knuckles on the table to underscore the seriousness of what he was saying. "You're completely gone."

"Gone, what do you mean, gone?" Lang mumbled absently.

"This is serious, Lang," Minkkinen continued breathlessly. "None of the serious papers want to write you up, not even the ones that Meriö owns. I can't even get you into the magazine questionnaires any more: My Favourite Books, My Life's Alphabet, Ten Things I Can't Live Without . . . they don't even want to use you there. The only thing I have is a phone call from Seiska. Apparently there's a rumour that you're sleeping with a teenage single mother in Berghäll."

"She's not a teenager, V.P.," Lang answered. "She's twenty-seven."

"Yes, yes. Whatever," Minkkinen said with irritation. "The point is you have to watch out."

"They smell blood?" Lang asked.

Minkkinen nodded. "I think so. We've had a pact, but they're prepared to break it. You are starting to become more interesting dirty than clean."

"I don't get it . . ." Lang started to mumble, then he stopped himself.

"What is it you don't get?" Minkkinen said and looked fiercely at Lang.

"Why does public life have to be dominated either by idolizing or black-listing?" Lang said. "Why isn't there any room for thinking in between?"

"Because man is lazy and mean," Minkkinen said cutting him off, then continuing, "Do you have anything we can give them? Something positive like a new book or . . . what about your boy? Isn't he about to graduate from high school? That could be an angle . . ."

"Stop it!" Lang said. "He graduated last year, he's living in London."

"You could of course be seen in public with a suitable female celebrity," Minkkinen said optimistically, ignoring him. "There are still some who would be willing to take a turn on the town with you. What about Mannila, for example, she's newly single and has a film release in December and . . ."

"What a goddamned media-whore you've become, V.P.!" Lang suddenly snarled. "I can't stand this shit any more! Here I am knocked out of the arena by children who roll around on the set half-drunk, as if they were skateboarding mentally. That's whenever they aren't busy showing their penises off to the press or insulting their guests. And then you want me – *me!* – to crawl for the same newspapers who worship these twenty-year-old raisin brains! Never! Not on your life, V.P., not on your life!"

"Listen to me, Kride," Minkkinen said patiently. "We're losing viewers to these young children and . . ."

"I don't give a shit!" Lang interrupted, "I am a thinking person and not a machine designed to interpret public reaction and react accordingly."

"Yes," Minkkinen said with a sudden chill in his voice, "you are a person who thinks far too much and doesn't get his butt in gear. Is it the chick who's done this to you?"

"This conversation is absurd," Lang said angrily and then continued with a rhetorical question. "Which one of us has lost his mind, V.P.?"

"I have no doubts on that point whatsoever," Minkkinen said haughtily. "You have, Lang."

"Crazy or not," Lang said in a tired voice. "I'm leaving. Good day to you, Mr Producer."

"Fine. Go," Minkkinen muttered when Lang got up, took his

coat and walked to the door. "Go on, you damned coward. It's still me who has to take the shit."

That same evening, at twilight, Lang sat at a window table at Carousel down by Havshamnen Harbour. He saw the October sky flare up and then die out behind Drumsö, and he saw the moon hang like a pale yellow scythe above the low warehouses at Busholmen. And he thought: V.P. is no longer my friend. V.P. has turned into a termite, another termite eating away at my soul.

When it was dark he did not go home, but to the office he rented on Villagatan. While he was waiting for the computer to connect to the server he thought about the fact that it had been a long time since he had been in here trying to write. There were three new messages in his e-mail account: a conciliatory one from V.P. Minkkinen, a worried one from Anni – she said that she had spoken to Johan on the phone and he had "sounded in bad shape" – and one from Sarita with the subject heading "are you really never going to answer?" Lang started by sending two lines to Minkkinen: "Possessing an acute perception is not the same as being mad. But sometimes possessing an acute perception can *drive* you mad." Then he wrote a long, friendly letter to Anni, whom he had not talked to for more than a year, and asked her to send more information about Johan. Lastly he erased Sarita's e-mail without reading it, then went to the Recycle Bin and emptied it. He, Christian Lang, was not one to buckle under pressure.

XVI

On a chilly, blustery Wednesday evening only about a week after the quarrel with Minkkinen, Lang came home after taping yet another weak instalment of "TBH". The rain poured down, the wind tore impatiently at the half-bare deciduous trees and all parks and spaces were in deep shadow. The occasional figure in black or brown walked quickly and unhappily along the abandoned streets and gave Helsinki the look of an old Fritz Lang film where all the murderers have been let out on probation at the same time. It was late and the parking spaces were all filled and Lang was forced to park up by Villa Ensi. He walked the few hundred metres up to Skarpskyttegatan with the rain and north wind in his face and a vague, unpleasant sensation in the back of his head: the suspicion that someone was following him. When he unlocked the door in the iron frame and took the first few steps across the little courtyard and saw the tall man in the duffel coat leaning against the far wall his heart started thumping with terror: Lang was sure he had finally come across his first stalker and that he was now about to die. The man in the duffel coat remained where he was, waiting. Lang approached the door with his keys ready in one hand and his other hand curled into a fist. He noted that the duffel-coat man was thin and long-haired: if he weren't a stalker you would take him for an addict looking to scrape up money for his next dose. Lang prepared to slip through the door quickly and shut it before the stranger had a chance to follow him through. It was only when the man was a few metres away that something about the ragged figure made him rethink and hazard: "Johan?"

And then at once he saw that the stranger was as terrified as he was and out of the semi-darkness by the wall there came a frightened and equally hesitant "Dad?"

Together Lang and Anni made the necessary arrangements for Johan to be admitted to a detox clinic in northern Esbo. It was the first time in more than ten years that the two of them had cooperated on anything. The fragile peace was necessary: Johan had developed a taste for both Ecstacy and amphetamines during his year in London and he was, it turned out, in exactly as bad a state as Anni had feared.

Lang's worry about Johan distracted him from thinking about Sarita for a while, and he continued, like a sleepwalker, to ignore her attempts to contact him. He became even more absent-minded in his professional life and there was no question now that the rift between him and V.P. Minkkinen had deepened and solidified. Speculation now centred on whether the "Blue Hour" team would manage to stay together until the end of May when the last show was scheduled to be taped and broadcast.

And then there was Anni. For the first time in over a decade, Lang saw the mother of his only child as a real person, not as an intelligent bitch who made caustic comments to him over the phone. When they divorced after eleven stormy years they had been thoroughly tired of each other and Anni had also been bitter about Lang's – numerous, as it turned out – infidelities. The little communication they had in the years that followed was only for Johan's sake, so that he would retain contact with both parents even though he lived with Anni and her new family. But now Anni and Lang ate two lunches and a dinner out alone, just the two of them, in the space of a few weeks. And even though these meetings were devoted to the topic of how they could best save Johan, Lang couldn't help thinking about Anni.

He noticed that both her spoken and written Swedish had deteriorated over the years. The three children she had with her new husband – a hard-working lawyer – spoke virtually no Swedish. Anni herself was an information manager at a large drug company: so the language of both her private and professional life was almost exclusively Finnish. Lang saw in his mind's eye how Anni's cool, elegant shell would melt when they made love. He remembered her love-talk, the broken, greedy snatches of words as she neared orgasm and he wondered if she said them in Finnish nowadays: probably. He wondered if Anni sometimes felt the way he did, that the thoroughly bilingual person loses her innermost self, that she no longer has a language for her deepest love and her deepest emotions, and that she therefore experiences all words spoken during the act of love as false and wrong, as if she wished there were a language that fitted somewhere *in between*. Lang wanted to ask Anni about all this, but he didn't dare. It seemed too intimate.

Lang also noticed how beautiful Anni had become. She was beautiful in a sharply-defined and mature way, which, when accompanied by the calm of a successful career and happy marriage, emerged as wholly natural and made Lang from time to time almost speechless. He sensed that Anni's beauty in his eyes was enhanced by the bond they had once shared and by the fact that they had had and cared for Johan together. Suddenly he felt he realized that he and Anni could well have continued to live together and love each other if they had only had a little more patience and taken more care in those years when they reached thirty. And as he was thinking all of these beautiful thoughts about Anni, the memory of Sarita suddenly seemed like something sharp and anxiety-ridden and incomplete. As he sat there on his restaurant chair and looked at his ex-wife, Lang imagined that he didn't miss Sarita, not the least little bit.

Lang visited Johan as often as he could in those weeks that Johan was at the clinic. Once, with the doctor's permission, they went in to Helsinki and had dinner at an Indian restaurant, but most of the time they simply took long walks on the autumn-wet roads in the clinic's neighbourhood. Sometimes when they walked together in the rain Lang recalled Sarita's words about how he was a person with a strong sense of duty and that he walked through crisis like a hard tight bundle and he wondered if he was as uneasy in his relationship to Johan now as he was with Estelle when she was sick. But he didn't think so, because he didn't feel any of the anger and irritation with Johan that so often coloured his feelings for Estelle.

Johan was full of regret and didn't say much; Lang had plenty of time for his own thoughts. Sometimes he walked beside his silent, saddened son who was nine centimetres taller than he was, and remembered images of a very different Johan. Again that November almost twenty years earlier, pushing the stroller through Hesperia Park, the rain that never ends. Johan sits up straight in the stroller, wearing the turquoise hat that ties under his chin and he laughs at everyone they pass. They slip into a café and buy some goodies and when they come home Johan splatters food on the walls and Lang gets angry. He suddenly sees with terrifying clarity his inadequacy as a father for the past twenty years. He could hear Anni's voice criticizing his child-rearing methods during their divorce. According to her it was a combination of a lax "do as you please" attitude that was interspersed with, from the child's perspective, completely incomprehensible, sudden explosions of anger when the strict upbringing Lang had received from Christel and Stig-Olof broke through his seemingly tolerant surface. And he could remember how hard it had been for him to choose the right level of familiarity with his son as when he called Johan after Anni had remarried, and Johan was already entering puberty. Should he say, "Hello, this is your father," or "Hi, it's Dad," or even "Kride, here"?

One day when Johan and he walked along the main road as usual and were on their way back to the clinic, Lang remembered a Christmas party at the daycare Tärnan. Johan had been wearing brown and white-painted cardboard and a tall, black paper hat: a completely adorable little gingerbread man. Lang sat with the other parents, his stomach tight because it was only a little after seven in the morning and gatherings always made him nervous and now he was starting to become A Famous Person and the other parents stared at him when they thought he wasn't looking. When the Christmas dancing started, Johan came over and said shyly, "Will you come and dance, Dad?" and Lang had reacted in totally the wrong way. Instead of being happy and proud over his little gingerbread man, now with the additional accessories of magic wand and wizard's hat, he became embarrassed and ill at ease and said, "No, Johan, not right now." Johan turned his head and looked at the other, jolly dads dancing together with their gingerbread men, lucia-maids, angels and Wise Men. One of the dads even had a video camera that he took turns pointing at his son and then at himself. Johan looked again at his dad, bit his lip and walked away. A little later Lang saw him with an angel and a Wise Man who didn't have any parents or family there.

As they were walking in through the front gate and down the long drive, Lang couldn't stop himself from asking Johan if he remembered the Christmas party at Tärnan. Johan listened carefully to his father's story.

"No, I don't remember it," he said. "I don't remember very much from when I was little. I remember more from middle school when you and Mom were always fighting in the evenings."

Then Johan was quiet for a while, and Lang too, until he noticed that Johan was laughing; a quiet, almost giggle-like laugh that grew in volume as they walked towards the clinic.

"What are you laughing at?" Lang said.

"At the fact that you think I started taking drugs because you didn't dance the Christmas dances with me at daycare! Come on, Dad!" Johan said, and now he was laughing so hard that even Lang had to smile. It was at that moment, he told me, that he knew Johan was going to be alright, that he would rejoin the sphere of the functioning human being.

Lang met Anni yet one more time. It was in the beginning of December and they had an early Christmas lunch to celebrate the fact that Johan was gradually getting better. Lang was still shaken by Johan's crisis and after a few glasses of wine he told Anni about the rejected gingerbread man and about the sense that he, Lang that is, had been flying through life like a spear, refusing to be a whole, feeling person. Anni reacted toughly. She was, Lang claimed bitterly, the kind of person who always accepted her own episodes of sentimentality but never those of others, and now she said sternly to him that his self-pity wasn't going to help anyone, not him, not her and above all not Johan, and then she rounded out her speech by reminding him that she had been telling him for years to dump his false and wearisome role as charismatic celebrity.

That evening Lang came home to Skarpskyttegatan still numb

from Anni's savage critique. When he heard a message from Sarita on the answering machine he listened to the end and then called her. Neither of them said very much. Sarita seemed almost speechless to hear from him. They met at a bar in the corner of Kajsaniemigatan and Berggatan shortly before midnight and there Sarita put her thin hand with the long fingers in his and said seriously, "I'm sorry."

"I'm sorry too," Lang mumbled in reply. Afterwards he remembered that a no! no! no! had been ticking inside him, but he was starved for love and he went home with her. Once he came in the door he walked over to the sleeping Miro and stroked him cursorily on the head. Then he walked around the apartment and opened all the wardrobe doors, then he went over to the window but ignored the TV-watcher with his outstretched legs and bare feet on the footstool in the apartment across the courtyard. Instead he looked around to make sure that no-one who didn't belong was hanging around down there. Only when these rituals had been completed did he go to the front door and put on the chain. But nothing helped. Lang still thought he could smell someone else's aftershave and he started to calm down only when Sarita told him that she hadn't seen Marko since the beginning of October and that Marko loved Miro and would never come over and make trouble when the boy was at home and lay sleeping.

All night and in the morning Lang refrained from saying "Why?" and neither he nor Sarita talked about the future. However, Lang did take his own small revenge, he told me, by not making love to Sarita immediately. Instead he shifted so that his body's position in relation to her mouth was a clear signal that she should take his member between her lips. While she did so he stroked her hair, started running his fingers through it, and finally pulled hard on it. It was only in the morning that the actual reconciliation occurred. Even though they heard that Miro was awake and watching TV, Lang slid down under the covers and buried his face between Sarita's legs until she started to shake and twitch, once, twice, three times until her body twisted in a silent struggle. Then they finally made love, and when Sarita sat on him Lang could see the thoughts and feelings move in her eyes. He saw fear and strength and suspicion and he saw in equal parts desire and pity, but now he saw no glint of laughter; the time of joking was past. And then he closed his eyes and it occurred to him when he really thought about it that he was prepared to do almost anything for Sarita. Because it was she, and not Anni and not anyone else, who had given him his life back.

XVII

Every time Lang stepped into Sarita's apartment he was reminded of his fear of Marko. It didn't help that the fear was mixed with a large dose of jealousy. Already a few days before Christmas he suggested that they pack her bag and spend a couple of nights at his newly-renovated apartment; Miro could sleep on the sofa, he said. But Sarita never agreed, saying Miro categorically refused. Which was true, because Lang had picked Miro up from school the day before Independence Day and they had discussed the matter and Miro had been adamant: he lived at Helsingegatan and sometimes spent the night in Stensvik and the summers in Virdois and that was that. Lang noticed that Miro didn't talk about Marko-daddy any longer and didn't say Uncle Chrisshan. Now that he had started school he used their first names only. Lang said to me later that there was a certain kind of child who grew up alone and was filled with adult thoughts at an early stage. These children took on a sapient and melancholy air which, Lang said, always made him think about how ordinary and secure his own childhood had been, despite the periodic coldness of his home. He thought that Miro the first-grader was on his way to becoming just such a precocious and unhappy child.

*

Apart from this, the weeks leading up to Christmas were characterized by Sarita and Lang's fumbling attempts to build a new sense of trust out of the ruins of the past. It was difficult: the prognosis was unsure and nothing was as it had been. There was even a new mood to their sex games; technically, they remained the same, but they were slower now and there was something new in Sarita's manner, something that most of all resembled a fragile desperation. Sometimes she uttered a "Your cock! Oh, your cock!" with her eyes closed, but without Lang being sure that she was really *there* and that it was *his* cock she was beseeching. In general Lang thought Sarita was more serious than before, perhaps also softer. Sometimes she cried at night, not bitterly but sadly, and with a sense of relief as if a weight had been lifted from her shoulders now that she no longer had to hide anything, but still got to keep Lang, a Lang who now knew he was involved in a mysterious *ménage à trois*.

After a while the questions came out. They came mainly from Lang who felt that answers and remorse were owing to him, and who was moreover immoderately proud of the fact that he had not slept with anyone during the four months of their separation. He didn't mention the fact that he had felt an extreme lust for his ex-wife Anni for half of October and most of November.

Sometimes Lang wanted to ask her point blank "Why?" But then he remembered Sarita's rhetorical "Haven't you ever been bewitched by anyone?" from their weekend trip to the little country town, and stopped himself. Instead he asked her about a detail that had continued to puzzle him; why she and Marko had put the chain on the door that day in August when they knew – or thought they did – that both Miro and Lang had left town.

"It was Marko," Sarita said reluctantly. "It had to do with some business of his. He was afraid, he said that *they* were after him.

And when I asked who *they* were, he said it would be better for me the less I knew."

"Do you know what it is he d—" Lang started to ask, but Sarita looked anxiously at him and interrupted,

"Never mess with Marko, Chrisshan! Don't start poking into his affairs, promise me that!"

But despite this conversation, and despite the fact that Lang in future made no secret of his dislike for Marko and his fear that he would suddenly turn up, he never managed to convince Sarita to promise not to have any more contact with her ex-husband. She only answered, "How on earth would I be able to promise anything like that? He's Miro's father, of course I have to have contact with him."

Sarita, Miro and Lang spent Christmas with Sarita's mother Virpi and her husband Heikki in Tampere. Lang wanted to bring the car, but Miro felt that one should take the train at Christmas. Sarita agreed and so they chose an intercity train filled to bursting, scheduled to leave on the afternoon of the 23rd. Virpi and Heikki lived in a two-bedroom apartment in a four-unit building not far from Sorsapuisto. Lang and Sarita stayed in the spare room to the left of the entry way, while Miro slept with his grandmother: Heikki had kindly offered to sleep on the sofa. When they unpacked their bags Lang saw a medium-large wrapped package in Sarita's luggage that had a card with the words "To My Dear Miro from Marko-daddy" in large but surprisingly beautiful handwriting. Lang wanted to ask what was in it but restrained himself.

Virpi and Heikki were cheerful and polite and a little curious about Lang because of his celebrity status. When Heikki had downed a few, he couldn't conceal the fact that he thought the show "The Blue Hour" and the TV personality Christian Lang somewhat pretentious: Heikki himself was an insurance inspector, had season tickets to the Tappara hockey games and had not once in the past five years missed a single episode of the quality soap opera "Our Street" on Channel 1. On Christmas Eve, when they had opened all the presents and Heikki and Lang sat boozing on the TV-sofa, Sarita's mobile rang from deep within her handbag that was hanging on the door handle between the kitchen and the living room.

"Your phone!" Lang shouted to Sarita who was in the kitchen with Virpi, loading plates and glasses into the dishwasher.

"Could you get it – my hands are so greasy," Sarita answered and added, "It's probably Kirsi, she promised to call around seven."

Lang got up and reluctantly started to dig in Sarita's bag. He found the phone, punched the talk button, held the Nokia 3210 to his ear and said,

"Hello."

At first there was no voice on the other end, then Marko said,

"So you're with them, Lang. Sarita said nothing about that."

Lang didn't answer. He walked into the kitchen and handed the phone to Sarita without a word. He walked back into the living room without bothering to stay and listen to the conversation. After a while Sarita came out of the kitchen, gave Lang a tired look, then handed the phone to Miro who was playing NHL 2000: Marko's parcel had contained a PlayStation console and two games.

"Hi, Marko," Miro said in a neutral voice. He listened carefully while Marko said something on the other end.

"Course it's great," Miro said after a while. "I'm Dallas and I'm playing Colorado. It's great. Thanks a lot."

Then it was Marko's turn to say something. Miro again listened carefully and when his father had finished he asked:

"Where are you, Marko?" Some more listening and then, "What are you doing there?"

Lang suddenly saw the sadness and longing in Miro's eyes. He felt a lump in his throat and excused himself to go and have a pee. Only a few drops came out and he realized he had gone away so that the others wouldn't see his reaction to the conversation between the boy and his father. When he finished in the bathroom he pulled on his coat and left the apartment. There, in the dim light from the street lamp, in the stillness of the holiday calm, he took out his mobile and dialled Anni's number. To Lang's surprise it was Johan who answered, even though he was shy and didn't normally answer at other people's houses. When they had wished each other a Merry Christmas, Lang delicately asked about his son's plans and Johan said he was intending to move back to London right after the New Year.

"Do you have to?" Lang asked. "What if you fall back in your old ways?"

"I won't, Dad. I'm smarter than that now."

They talked a while longer and Lang promised to call again on New Year's Day. Before he went back in, he called his mother and Uncle Harry. When he had finished talking to Uncle Harry he asked to speak to Estelle who had been released from hospital only a few weeks before and who had immediately moved in with Harry and Marie.

"Alas Estelle has a terrible cold and she has gone to bed already," Harry said. "Would you like me to wake her?"

"No, there's no need," Lang said feeling relieved. "Tell her I'll call back another day."

In the days between Christmas and New Year Lang finally convinced Sarita and Miro to spend a few nights at his apartment. But the experiment did not turn out well because even though Miro had brought along his PlayStation console and even received Lang's permission to play indoor hockey in the living room, he constantly complained of being bored and how he wanted to go home. Sarita didn't seem to feel comfortable either. She was restless and distant and tore at her cuticles while they watched TV in the evenings. She even picked at her cuticles the night they watched "Some Like It Hot", which they had borrowed from the Classics shelf at the local video shop. She didn't smile once, despite Monroe, Lemmon and Curtis's best efforts and even though Lang almost split his seams laughing at the film that he and I usually saw every summer at the Bio Rix in the suburb where we lived.

Sarita, Miro and Lang were back in the apartment on Helsingegatan before New Year's Eve. Marko had returned in time to see in the new millennium and wanted to have Miro with him out at Stensviken for the weekend. After several telephone conversations Sarita had managed to get Marko to promise that he would stay sober and take Miro to Helsinki and up on Observatory Hill to look at the city's huge firework display, planned down to the last detail by an expert team flown in from Japan. Lang and Sarita spent the evening at a large party in V.P. Minkkinen's new penthouse apartment in Gräsviken. Minkkinen was also showing off his new girlfriend who was twenty-two, blonde and slender. She hosted a new and very popular adventure show called "The Precipice", on Channel 3. The party was chaotic and raucous, the mood hysterically elevated and Lang felt extremely uncomfortable. A few middle-aged women who he knew to be reporters for the weekly magazines stared curiously at him and Sarita all evening, while his and Minkkinen's millennium embrace at the stroke of twelve was dutiful and cool. Lang heard the enormous firework show thunder distantly across the Kronberg Bay and he heard the sharper, higher sounds from all the home-bought fireworks being let off from all the backyards and shores in Gräsviken. Suddenly he felt he had drunk more than enough champagne and didn't want to take another puff of his fat Cohiba cigar. He thought about all the useless millennium year trinkets that would be scattered all around tomorrow morning and that no-one would even so much as look at them any more and then he looked questioningly at Sarita and inclined his head to the door. Sarita smiled, wiggled her half-empty champagne glass in a meaningful way and took a long, pleasurable puff of her thin cigarillo that she was smoking through a holder inlaid with false mother-of-pearl: she had no desire to leave at all.

At the end of January, Lang and V.P. Minkkinen flew to Stockholm. They had each booked a single room at Sergel Plaza and then spent a few days in talks with an international production company who ran an affiliated office in one of the skyscrapers at Hötorget. The talks were about the possibility of selling the "TBH" format, complete with host. Minkkinen had in his letters to the production company stressed the fact that Lang was actually a Swedish-speaking Finn and could therefore do "TBH" in Sweden as well as Finland. He had conjured up a vision where Lang's persona would create the same media impact and have the same exotic breakthrough power as the Swedish-speaking Finnish television personalities Jörn Donner and Mark Levengood had had in earlier decades. This idea was probably, Lang wrote in one of his letters from prison, best viewed as Minkkinen's last attempt to save their dying friendship, extravagant and generous as he was.

But the Stockholm trip was a failure and after four fruitless days Lang called Sarita from Sergel Plaza only a few hours before his flight home. To his surprise, not to mention disappointment, Sarita did not sound keen to see him. She had a cold, she said, and moreover she was exhausted from working overtime at the studio: she wanted to be home alone with Miro a few more nights. Lang could come and stay with her the following week. Lang's jealousy was immediately aroused. He refused to end their conversation, he was seductive and insistent and finally succeeded in getting Sarita to promise to have dinner with him later the same evening. They met at half past nine at a Thai restaurant in Tölö. Sarita was wearing more make-up than she normally did and she was wearing a bright red jumper with a polo neck and wide-legged jeans in another, almost as strong shade of red. Even so Lang's first impression of her was that she had told the truth; she did look tired and as if she had a cold. The make-up couldn't hide her pallor and the dark rings under the eyes. Lang, however, felt upbeat and tender and horny after the long and frustrating days of meetings and during the dinner he caressed her hands and cheeks repeatedly and leaned over to kiss her and tried to put his tongue in her mouth, although she seemed absent-minded and uninterested in these displays of affection or longing. Lang was stubborn and patient, and then the evening ended with them taking a taxi back to Helsingegatan. When they came into the apartment Kirsi, who had been baby-sitting Miro, looked at Lang as if he represented all that was rotten and wrong with close to three billion men. A little later, when Kirsi was getting ready to leave, she embraced Sarita and whispered something in her ear. Lang pricked up his own ears and thought it sounded like a question. But Sarita didn't whisper anything in return, she simply shrugged her shoulders and opened the door for Kirsi, who disappeared into the darkness of the stairwell. When Lang came out of the bathroom a few moments later Miro was sleeping calmly in his alcove. Sarita had already gone into the bedroom and drawn the curtains, taken off her clothes and climbed into bed. All the lights were off. When Lang started to stroke her body and at the same time fumbled for the light switch of the reading lamp, Sarita took his hand and asked him to leave it off.

When they had finished making love, she cried softly and asked him to leave. She wanted to sleep alone, she said, and wake up alone in the morning. Lang already had his suspicions. When he got up to get a glass of water from the kitchen he quickly turned around and flicked the switch of the bedside lamp. Sarita was lying with the covers down around her hips and was taken by surprise; she didn't have time to pull anything over herself and Lang saw the big bruises with terrible clarity. There was one on each of her arms, a smaller one on her neck and he also saw the bright red mark on her stomach, just next to her navel: a burn mark. Then Sarita threw herself over him and started to hit him, hard, with clenched fists while she screamed at him with a wild and broken and desperate voice: "Off! Off! TURN IT OFF YOU GODDAMN BASTARD! AND GET THE HELL OUT OF HERE!"

Lang quickly turned off the light. Sarita stopped hitting him and got up and pulled on a big white T-shirt and walked to the window and lit a cigarette. But she was still crying and now Miro had woken up and wanted to join her: there were soft, tip-toeing steps and then he was there in the door, crying up a storm. Lang began trying to convince him to return to the sleep alcove in the other room, with calming assurances. It took about ten minutes, or perhaps fifteen, but eventually he managed to calm the boy. Miro lay sobbing in his bed while Lang stroked his hair. Then he fell asleep. After that Lang's leadership suddenly abated. He walked back into the bedroom and sat on the side of the bed for a long time. He had his socks in his hands and he didn't know what he should do. Sarita was still at the window. She smoked another cigarette and when it was finished she said with a strangled voice, "You don't understand, Lang. You understand absolutely nothing, so go away and leave me alone."

"If I go now, will he come here tonight?" Lang said.

"No, he won't be here tonight. Please leave," Sarita said exhaustedly.

And Lang finally did as she asked: he put his clothes on and left.

XVIII

Lang's body ached in the morning, both from the blows and the words that Sarita had aimed at him. *You understand absolutely nothing.* He took a day off work and tracked down Kirsi the hair stylist at her place of work, which was a successful modelling agency. He asked her – "for Sarita's sake" – to tell him all she knew about Marko, about who he was, what circles he moved in and what was going on between him and Sarita. Kirsi seemed to regret that she had glared at him the previous evening as if he were simply Marko's successor; this day she was very friendly. But she also said she had only known Sarita for six years or so and that Marko's and Sarita's story had begun long before that.

"I know," Lang said. "And I want it to end now."

"Unfortunately there's not much chance of that," Kirsi said. "Sarita has tried to leave him a few times. Once there was even a restraining order. But she's always pulled back to him."

"Why?" Lang asked helplessly, and Kirsi said she didn't know. She just knew that their relationship had been complicated from the start and had only grown worse and worse. Then she added:

"Sarita doesn't tell me much either."

Lang asked a few more questions and Kirsi gave only vague answers and said she was sorry she couldn't be of more help. She said that in all other respects Sarita was a competent and rational person who was fully capable of taking care of herself and of making good decisions. Marko must have some kind of hold on Sarita, but Kirsi didn't know what it was. But she was sure on one point: she didn't think Sarita's relationship with Lang would help – quite the opposite, in fact. Marko could be decent, Kirsi said, but if she had interpreted Sarita's cryptic remarks correctly he was being impossible right now, and that was due to Lang.

"Why don't you save your own skin, why don't you get out of this?" she then said, and before Lang had a chance to reply she went on, "Those two belong together, don't you understand? They belong together even though they don't want to and there's nothing you can do about it. Pull out now, Lang, before anything worse happens."

She looked at him ironically and, Lang thought, somewhat covetously as if weighing her chances of bagging him after Sarita. But then she said, "You can't, can you, Lang? You love her, don't you?"

Later that same day Lang called Marko's mother in Stensvik on his mobile. He had seen her last name and number in Sarita's phone book and had memorized both. But this manoeuvre didn't yield anything either. He presented himself as "Tero", an old friend of Marko's from school. To his relief the mother, who had a high and somewhat anxious tone of voice, didn't ask any difficult questions about which class he had been in or if he had played in the same hockey team as Marko. Instead she sounded almost frightened when she said she had no idea where her son was these days, that he seemed swallowed up by the earth and that it was no good calling her about him because Marko only saw her very occasionally.

When Sarita called Lang a few days later, sounding gentle and remorseful, Lang didn't pretend to be either hurt or play hard to get. She invited him over for a dinner of reconciliation and he immediately got into the Celica and drove to Berghäll. Sarita met him downstairs on the street and they embraced, staying like that for a long time and Lang felt the warmth of her body stream through his. There was no longer a place for explanations, he said to me, those should all have come earlier – a lot earlier, he felt intuitively as he stood there in the doorway and hugged her.

On the surface everything was the same. Sarita took the number 8 tram to the studio where she worked. Lang went on running "TBH" into the ground. He continued picking Miro up from school on Wednesdays. Physically he continued to desire Sarita as much as before, but it was hard to reestablish the same ease between them. Instead, he said, they started to resemble two survivors of a shipwreck clinging onto each other in the absence of life supports. Sarita in particular had changed. The hard-boiled irony that had been so characteristic of her when they first met was almost completely gone. In its place was a sensitive, unbearably tense person who longed for love instead of the hell in which she was currently living. Lang now noticed to his consternation that Sarita reminded him of Estelle when she cried, that the corners of her mouth twitched in the same way as Estelle's. He also realized he had for a long time stubbornly blinded himself to Sarita's weakness. He sensed that he had disavowed this fragility in order to be able to continue mystifying her as woman, and his bad conscience on this point allowed him quickly to repress the uncomfortable parallels to Estelle. He now gave himself the task of loving Sarita more than before, more than he had ever loved another person.

Lang soon tired of the compulsive and humiliating ritual involving searching through all the wardrobes and casting frightened glances down into the courtyard and checking that the chain was on the door. He asked Sarita straight out: does Marko have a key to the apartment, yes or no? Sarita avoided his gaze and continued emptying the dishwasher and Lang interpreted her silence as a yes. That same week he forced through changing all the locks. He called the locksmith himself and asked him not only to change the existing locks but to install an extra security lock and then he supervised the work one afternoon when Sarita was at the studio. Sarita didn't raise a word of protest against this project, but neither did she seem relieved. That first night with the new locks – which was also the first night without the chain on – Lang kept sweating and had trouble falling asleep, and in a moment of weakness he discovered himself thinking that Sarita's indifference was perhaps an indication that Marko was a man who could pick any lock he liked.

One Wednesday in the middle of March Lang did an instalment of "The Blue Hour" with a strong emphasis on pop culture. "TBH" had for a long time had a structure with two parts. During the first half-hour Lang had two or three guests who talked about a broadly assigned topic while he moderated the discussion, while in the second half of the show he tried to dig into a chosen guest's life and work. The show concluded with Lang in front of the camera doing a three-minute sarcastic monologue about some current event. This Wednesday Lang was first scheduled to talk with the film stars Irina Björklund and Laura Malmivaara about what it was like to do sex scenes on the silver screen and after a short break he would take on the scarred singer-legend Dave Lindholm. The live audience was made up of students from a technical college in Esbo and literature students from Helsinki University. All went according to plan. Lang's introduction was one of his punchiest in a long time and the flirty, somewhat suggestive conversation with Björklund and Malmivaara flowed smoothly. But then there was a break in the taping. The whole studio space was lit up by strong lights and Lang and his guests could now look out into the audience which during taping appeared as dark silhouettes seated at the small restaurant tables towards the back. While Björklund and Malmivaara were helped out of their microphones and stood up to give their places to Lindholm, Lang looked out routinely and calmly over the audience and suddenly he was staring straight into Marko's cold, grey eyes.

Lang broke into a panic. His old compulsive thought about a stalker popped up again: he was about to die, and the man who would do the deed was Marko. There was an internal struggle: he wanted to cut short the taping of the show due to acute nausea. He wanted to expose Marko to the crowd, stand up out of his chair and point to the uninvited guest and shout: there is the man who abuses my beloved. Someone call the police! He wanted to assemble V.P.Minkkinen and the whole crew and ask them who was responsible for making sure that unauthorized visitors didn't manage to sneak into the studio audience. He wanted to yell at them, every last one. But Lang didn't do any of these things. Instead he completed the recording of the show. However, he was absentminded and lacked concentration while he interviewed Dave Lindholm and he was pale and tense and faltered several times during the closing monologue, which was about what a pseudo-event the millennium-craze had turned out to be, now that they were three months into the year 2000.

When the show was over and the studio was once again bathed in light Lang looked to the place where Marko had been sitting, but it was empty. He called Minkkinen over and told him in a tight voice that there had been an intruder in the audience and that he wanted to have a meeting with whoever was responsible to assure himself that it wouldn't happen again.

"How do you know that he did not have a ticket?" Minkkinen

said, and Lang hesitated for a moment. How did he know Marko wasn't a student of a technical college in Esbo or of the humanities at Helsinki University? But then he decided that neither explanation was likely.

"Believe me, I know," he said to Minkkinen, then turned on his heel and walked on shaky legs down to the cantina. He had a cup of tea, ate a sandwich and felt humiliated, crushed. The studio where "TBH" was filmed was Lang's country: now that he no longer wrote novels and didn't create his own fictitious worlds, the studio – with its dramatic and constantly changing lighting, and its steady stream of guests following each other in an endless circuit – was the only place in the world where he was sovereign, where he and no-one else was the central figure, whose whims and mood everyone had to kowtow to. And now the borders of this country had been violated, the self-determination of Langland had been called into question and the fragility of its defences had been revealed. When Lang took the lift down to the car park he was still shaken. He sat behind the wheel of the Celica, backed out of his parking space, put the car in first and was about to accelerate up the ramp when he saw a sudden movement to the right. The passenger door opened and Marko slid in, unhurried, smooth, and said, "I'm on my way into town, Lang. Why don't you give me a lift."

It was raining. The first few minutes when they were driving out of east Böle and along Nordenskiöldsgatan towards Tölö, Lang was simply paralysed by his fear and could not get a word out. Marko didn't say anything either. He sat there humming to himself, and occasionally made a satisfied, smacking sound. When they were stopped at a red light outside Aurora Hospital, Marko said slowly and thoughtfully,

"So you had her change the locks, did you, Lang?"

His voice made Lang shiver, but he controlled himself and said, as coldly as he could manage, "What do you want, Marko? What do you want from Sarita? And what do you want from me?"

"I'm Miro's father," Marko said. "And I'm Sarita's husband. Shouldn't I be the one asking you the questions?" He made a pause for effect, then imitated Lang's voice and said, "What do you want, Christian? What do you want of Sarita?"

"That's a load of shit," Lang said, furious. "You're not her husband. You two are divorced."

"On paper," Marko said. "You're a writer, Lang. You should know how lightly formalities weigh in relation to flesh and desire and blood."

Lang was silent. For a few minutes all that was heard was the monotone swoosh of the windscreen wipers and the low drone of the engine.

"I think it's time we got to know each other, you and me," Marko said lightly. "I didn't think you would go back to her after what happened in August, but you did, Lang. You surprised me."

"I know what you do to her, Marko," Lang said.

"Oh, you know," Marko said without a trace of concern. "That's good, because I don't."

They continued on in silence past Mannerheimvägen, past the tram depots and the Old Trade Fair and the National Opera. Lang tried to concentrate on the rush-hour traffic but was aware the whole time of the physical threat, the evil energy that kindled and sparked from Marko.

"They say you're finished, Lang," he said smiling when they were waiting at a red light by the National Museum. "They say you're finished and that 'TBH' is going off the air."

"Who are these 'they'?" Lang tried to sound as ironic and feather-light as his opponent.

"It's just something I heard," Marko said unflustered. "You should have me on your show, Lang. In that second bit, where you go deeper. I've seen a thing or two, see. I would have a lot to talk about."

"Really," Lang said, "What would you have to talk about?"

"War," Marko said. "I've killed, Lang. Both men and women. How about you, by the way? Didn't want to do your military service? Chose to serve in a civil capacity? Some hospital in the '80s?"

"Don't give me that," Lang said, getting over into the bus lane and accelerating angrily past the state building. "You came back with your tail between your legs. They didn't want you. Too unstable, a liability. Sarita told me."

"Did she, now," Marko smiled. "And are you sure she's telling you the truth? Did it ever occur to you she might be trying to make things look a bit better than they are? Because I don't think Sarita likes to think of the father of her only child as a killer, do you?"

Lang shook his head, but he didn't say anything. He slowed down for a red light by the Forum crossing and then Marko opened his door and said, "I'm getting off here. Thanks for the lift, Lang." He jumped out of the Celica in one supple movement, slipped between two cars and disappeared into the crowd on Simonsgatan.

XVIIII

Later that same evening when Lang told Sarita what had happened he wanted her to comfort him and say it was nothing, that Marko had just been playing around. But instead Sarita became frightened and fluttery. She asked Lang to tell his story again and again, she asked countless questions about what Marko's manner and his tone of voice had been and what he had actually said, as if she thought she would be able to extract some hidden meaning – somehow blocked for Lang – from this event that she had not even been witness to. Lang realized that Sarita was just as scared as he was, perhaps even more so, and this realization only further fuelled his fear.

Despite all the information I have gathered over time, and despite the effort I have put into this story and above all into understanding Lang's motive, it still puzzles me that he didn't try harder to extract himself that final spring. Sarita's friend Kirsi had told him straight out to try to save his own skin. Marko's continued presence in Sarita's life had become more intrusive, his attitude to Lang more threatening. Sarita also signalled more and more often that her strength was gone and that there was really no hope for her and Lang's love. But even so Lang continued to confide in her and sleep with her, long after the most basic conditions for a viable relationship had crumbled away. Perhaps on an unconscious level he imagined that his fame would protect him from sorrows and catastrophes, the way that some really famous or really rich people sometimes imagine they can't get AIDS, or that they won't be held accountable for crimes they commit.

This isn't to say that Lang didn't make adjustments that spring. He would so dearly have loved to believe, he wrote bitterly from prison, that only he, Sarita and Miro had keys to the new locks that he had had installed in the apartment. But Lang had no such illusions and therefore he no longer spent the night at Helsingegatan. Instead they met during the day, had lunch a few times a week and then – if Sarita could spare a few hours from the studio – went to the apartment on Skarpskyttegatan and made love in Lang's bed. But in May Sarita repeatedly assured him that Marko had gone abroad again, this time for a longer period. These assurances subdued Lang's fear somewhat and now they started to meet more frequently. One night in May they left a downtown bar and took a road along the train yard and over Fågelsången and home to Sarita's. It was cold. Lang clearly remembered seeing the smoke rising thick and white from the power station chimneys in Sörnäs, as if it were winter. But the night sky was no longer a winter black; it was indigo, and suddenly Sarita pulled him over towards her and they stopped there on the path that ran along the east side of Tölö inlet, and they kissed. They stood there for a long time, in the heart of the city, surrounded on every side by the familiar landmarks: Finlandia House, Parliament, Kiasma, the Sanoma Building, the Cathedral, the labour organization building, Berghäll Church, the stadium tower. The whole city, in both its present and past guises, pulsed around them, but Lang only felt the moist heat and sweet alcohol taste in Sarita's mouth and the defiant warmth in both their bodies. Suddenly he remembered exactly how teenage girls' mouths used to taste:

chewing gum, tobacco, sweet liqueurs and cherry lip gloss. An image of Anni on their first date flashed through his mind. It had been in January, it was cold, he and Anni were both nineteen years old and had arranged to meet at a shabby bar in the Glass Palace. A huge white scarf was carelessly thrown around Anni's neck and she was wearing jeans so tight it looked as if she had been poured into them. But at once the image of Anni faded away and Lang instead remembered Sarita's story of how she and Marko would sleep with each other in the snow. Jealousy flamed up inside him, inciting his desire so that he kissed Sarita harder and bit her lower lip. A spark of merciless, youthful hunger for life went through Lang's body and he wanted to tell Sarita that they should lie down right there where they were standing, right there where the limp reeds from last year lay scattered along the shore, and they should do it in the chilly spring night, surrounded by the muffled roar of the city. But he didn't say anything of the sort. Instead he stopped in the middle of the kiss, and hugged Sarita even closer to him so that she ended up with her head against his shoulder, all without saying a word.

One Wednesday afternoon at the end of May Lang was contacted by the much talked-about, mythical network owner Meriö. The contact was mediated by a cross V.P. Minkkinen and consisted only of his telling Lang to send a message to a certain e-mail address. Minkkinen knew that the address belonged to one of Meriö's many private secretaries, and Lang became anxious. He did not know Meriö personally, they had only met in passing at a cocktail party a few years earlier and on top of this Lang had just wrapped up his penultimate and, in his opinion, utterly disastrous "TBH" instalment. He did not expect to be stroked by anyone at this point, least of all by Meriö. But to his surprise it turned out that Meriö wanted to invite him to dinner the following Tuesday.

Lang wrote accepting the invitation and said he was planning to come by car, and on Tuesday morning he received e-mail instructions directing him to a residential district in Esbo. On the way out he stopped at a petrol station in Ängskulla to fill up. In the café section a TV screen was tuned to a rerun of the most recent "TBH" show. Lang walked over to a corner and watched for a while and saw that what he had sensed during the taping was indeed true: first he had failed to get two famous dance artists to speak openly of their homosexuality, and then he had failed even more drastically to get the new president's husband Arajärvi to analyse at all interestingly the burdens and opportunities of his role.

The area in which Meriö lived was set apart from the rest of the community and was clearly a neighbourhood for the very rich: a handful of streets dotted with palatial villas, hidden behind silver firs, high walls and protected by video cameras and remote-controlled gates. Lang waited outside the closed gate of Meriö's property and after a while a man in a uniform appeared and asked for his identification. Then the gates opened and Lang drove the hundred metres up to the house. He was received by an efficient young woman, and he registered at the same time how quiet it was inside, but it was only when she showed him into the dining room that he understood no-one else was invited: the table was set for two.

Meriö's greying hair was long and pulled into a ponytail, as if the multimillionaire was trying to say that a hippie still lived within him. His handshake was firm and he said at once that he wanted them to call each other by their first names. Meriö was casually dressed in faded jeans and work boots, but his jacket looked exclusive and his watch had probably cost 20,000 marks or more, Lang thought. While they were waiting for their first course, Meriö complimented Lang on his novels. They were, said the network owner, like riddles or rebuses, full of asides and dead ends but still in a paradoxical way accessible thanks to the raw sensibility that coursed through them and gripped the reader even though he – and Meriö wanted to be quite honest on this point – didn't understand what they meant. Lang thanked Meriö for his perceptive words and then enquired if he could be so bold as to ask the pretext for the dinner invitation which came just as "TBH" was about to end its run. Meriö smiled wanly at Lang's polite phrases, but then his smile quickly faded and he said, "That's why, Christian. I wanted to meet you and talk to you before we go our separate ways, in all likelihood for ever. I happen to be of the persuasion that you could have gone on to great heights." He made a deliberate pause here, as if he wanted Lang to say something, protest, or perhaps ask "Why – didn't I reach them already?" But Lang waited and so Meriö continued, as at the same time he started to bite into the marinated crayfish tails that a young server had just placed in front of them.

"Perhaps I should add that I have followed you carefully for some time now. I am a member of the board and part owner of the company that publishes your books in Finnish, so I already had my eye on you when you became a TV host. And now, in order to answer the question you did not dare pose just a moment ago: no, you have not quite lived up to my expectations. But drink up, Christian! This wine is from a rather mediocre vineyard, but it is a good year. And eat, damn it. This is catering food – my cook is on holiday – but it's a family business and they do a good job."

Lang calmly picked up a crayfish tail and said, "Please don't leave me guessing, Rauno. I want you to explain how I have disappointed you." Lang then made his own deliberate pause and added with biting irony, "And I am dying to hear how *you* effected my literary breakthrough."

Meriö looked at Lang with amusement and took a good

amount of time before he replied. "The explanation is simple, really," he said. "You haven't managed to change with the times, move into the twenty-first century. You're mired in the old ways of thinking. Perhaps it's wrong of us to measure everything in speed and money, perhaps we're causing damage when we celebrate youth and quick-wittedness and make 'experience' synonymous with 'decrepitude'. It is also very possible that we are witness to a cultural decline. However, we have no choice but to observe the dominant structures and reigning mass psychology. To challenge these would cost an enormous amount of money and mean an enormous waste of human talent and technical resources. We have to be sensible, Christian, and I don't think the right thing to do is sit in the TV screen and try to convince everyone, from the prime minister to the latest techno-star, that everything was better in the olden days."

Lang chewed his crayfish tail thoughtfully and asked, "So that's all you think I do: whine?"

"During the last two seasons, yes," Meriö said. "You haven't held up under pressure. And as for your other question, about your literary breakthrough . . . let me just say that I have widespread interests even among the magazine press. There are many journalists who do not consider themselves above taking their cue from me."

While they ate the main course, exquisitely prepared turbot filets with an expensive but somewhat sweet Chardonnay, they changed the topic and talked instead about this and that and current social issues – such as the ever-increasing drug traffic from the east. The young woman serving them refilled their glasses generously and it was soon clear to Lang that he would not be able to drive home. It was only when they reached dessert – a *crème brulée* with a crust scorched and brittle in just the right way – that Meriö returned to the subject of Christian

Lang and the expectations he had awakened and failed to live up to.

"I hope you were not hurt by my honesty a while back, Christian," he said, "but every phenomenon has its time at the top and your time is over. I don't see any point in beating about the bush here. But I do want to know why you've changed. I tried to provoke you into speaking your mind, but I have not succeeded there."

"The explanation is simple, really," Lang smiled, taking a large spoonful of the sugar crust. "I've lost my taste for the world controlled by people like you. It is a world in which only gladiators and warriors can feel useful. It is a dictatorship. We are all, *all*, expected to step into the arena and greet the market economy with a humble 'Caesar, we who are about to die salute you'. The capital cities of the world are full of talented young people who do nothing but produce and consume useless goods and soulless entertainment. It's such a goddamned bore."

When Lang finished he saw that Meriö was smiling in a melancholy and inward way.

"Oh, yes," the network owner sighed after a few moments and signalled the server to bring the trolley with cognac, whisky and liqueurs. "You make me think of my youth, Christian. I was actually one of the activists, only for a short while, of course, but still . . ." Meriö's voice died away and he sank into thought. Lang waited. After a while Meriö looked up, met his eye and said, "You think it's going too fast? You want to get off?"

"Yes," Lang said. "I want to get off. I want something else, anything but this crazy chasing after absolutely nothing. I want to learn how to accept my tiredness and my doubts. I no longer want to be quick-witted and hard and cruel."

"A worthy goal," Meriö said and scrutinized a carefully sealed bottle of calvados that he had picked up from the trolley. He looked thoughtfully at Lang and added, as he handed the bottle to the server and indicated that she should open it, "But I don't suppose you will find it as easy to get off as you may think."

One of Meriö's employees drove Lang home to Skarpskyttegatan in a Volvo S80. It was two o'clock in the morning. When Lang woke up the following day it was late and he had a headache from too much wine, calvados and whisky. The keys to the Celica lay on his hall floor and beside them there was a note indicating where the car was parked.

A few hours later Lang taped the final instalment of "The Blue Hour". He looked pale and tired, but he was as poised and knowledgeable as ever. His guests on the first half of the show were the Minister of Foreign Affairs, Tuomioja, and a veteran historian of the Cold War. They discussed whether Finland was at risk of becoming as obsequious towards the European Union or the United States as the country had been towards the Soviet Union during Lang's – and my – youth. Lang's final guest was the singer and songwriter J. Karjalainen who had released a new album. Lang skilfully connected their talk to the debate before the break and he and Karjalainen talked at length about the strangely dualistic world they had grown up in, where many children and teenagers were small Americans while the country they lived in made pains to appear to be the Soviet Union's closest neighbour and friend. Everything flowed as it should and it was only in the last few minutes of "The Blue Hour"'s almost seven year lifespan that Lang allowed himself to loosen his grip a little. When he had thanked J. Karjalainen and expressed his appreciation to the viewers for their support and response during the last seven seasons he stood up and walked with firm steps to a spot in front of one of the cameras, for his last monologue. There was not a trace of the sarcastic tone that he had excelled at for so many years. Instead his final monologue became something of a disguised greeting to Meriö and V.P. Minkkinen. Without a hint of a tremble he spoke for three minutes in defence of empathy, thoughtfulness and depth of feeling, and his talk ended with Lang asking himself what his own responsibility was in a media world that had made impatient children even of those who, at least biologically speaking, were adults.

XX

Late one evening in the middle of July, Lang was walking across Skillnaden. The rainy and grey afternoon had turned into a blustery dusk and thereafter a chilly night, and all the while he had drifted from restaurant to restaurant and ordered a glass of wine and towards the end also a glass of sweet almond liqueur at each place. Lang shivered: the summer – the first of the millennium – had been frosty in all ways. This week Sarita was in Stockholm with Kirsi, while Miro had gone to his grandmother's cabin in Virdois. The week before Lang had spent with Sarita and Miro in another summer house, one they had rented by the shore of Lake Saimen, and it had not been a success. Miro had been stung in his neck by a bee and Sarita had complained that Lang's hands felt cold and clammy when he touched her. As always, he had desired her, but he could no longer deny to himself that the last year he had come to see her as more ordinary, more worn, more used up.

He turned around at the top of the hill and looked out over Mannerheimvägen. The north wind was cold and nippy. Three flags on the roof of Stockmann's smacked in the wind. The sun had already set, but the sky was still light and milky. It was a familiar sight: Lang had always thought his city beautiful in a cool and distant way, and he knew that it was exactly like this, with the lonely scattering of flags and a wind that penetrated skin and bone even in the middle of summer when the nights were shortest, that he would remember Helsinki, if he ever moved away.

A few minutes later Lang crossed Bangatan and continued along Skepparebrinken down towards Femkanten. He turned to the left and started to struggle up Skarpskyttegatan with the sharp wind in his face. Downtown there had been plenty of people despite the cold, but Skarpskyttegatan was almost deserted, apart from an idle flaneur in tracksuit trousers and a college sweatshirt, stopping to look in a shop window. It was a used-book shop that Lang considered low-ranking and he was tempted to ask what the man was looking at. Instead he passed him at arm's length and it was only when he was a few steps away that he heard him say quietly, "Hey there, Lang, I've been waiting for you," and realized it was Marko. Lang shivered with terror, but he resisted the impulse to run. He stopped and turned.

"What do you want from me, Marko?" he said evenly.

"Always the same question! And yet we meet so rarely," Marko said cheerfully, and went on: "It's time for us to have a drink together, you and me. My treat. Or would you rather have me over? Your place is right up here, isn't it?"

"I'd rather invite a scorpion," Lang muttered. "At least then I'd know what I was looking at." He hoped that he'd managed to conceal his terror and continued as succinctly as he could, "Where do you want to go?"

Marko shrugged. "Maxill?" he suggested.

"No, that's a damned fish bowl," Lang said.

"You're embarrassed to be seen out with me, in other words," Marko laughed.

"You can think what you like," Lang said tiredly and started walking back towards Femkanten. Marko walked beside him and asked in a kindly conversational tone, "So, how was the holiday?"

"Which damned holiday?" Lang said.

"The one at Lake Saimen," Marko said.

"It could have been better," Lang said. "But you probably knew that already."

They went to the cellar bar Temppeli in the corner of Ulrikasborgsgatan and Högbergsgatan. They stayed for barely an hour, until the bar closed, but during that time Marko let slip that he had been keeping his eye on Lang since the latter spent his first night at Sarita's. He asked if Lang remembered how he – Marko – had walked past while Lang was waiting down on Helsingegatan, waiting to be let in, almost two years ago. Their eyes had met, Marko said, could Lang really not recollect it? Lang searched in his memory. He recalled that the summer had been cold, even colder than this one. He remembered leaving the Celica at home and taking the tram, even though it bothered him that people recognized him and stared. He remembered being obsessed with the thought of Sarita, the memory of her deep navel that he had seen rise and fall with her breath as she lay on the sofa. But he had no recollection whatsoever of a Marko supposedly standing outside Sarita's door, nor of meeting his gaze. This is what he told Marko, who took a sip of beer and said thoughtfully, "Once last winter I stood in Sarita's doorway and saw you hugging. It was a beautiful sight. Idyllic. Then you had the locks changed, Lang. That wasn't very nice of you."

Lang tried to catch his eye, but failed.

"Why are you doing this, Marko?" he asked instead. "Why are you acting like this?" Marko looked straight ahead of him and said,

"It's very simple, Lang. I don't lie to myself like you do."

The following hour was spent at a beer hall on Stora Robertsgatan – when Lang described that evening for me he couldn't remember the name of the place – and at three o'clock they had squeezed next to the bar in the crowded Lost & Found. In the midst of his drunkenness Lang thought about the fact that even though he and Marko were rivals – enemies, in fact – this evening would nonetheless lead to rumours that Lang was a closet homosexual dating a younger man. The same second that Lang thought this Marko smiled and said, "Since everyone here assumes we're gay, which I'm sure they find interesting since you're a celebrity, I'll follow the script and suggest we go back to your place. Surely you have something to drink there, Lang? I won't rape you, I promise."

Lang looked at his new-found drinking buddy and said, "I'm no idiot, Marko. What do you have on you? A stiletto? A pen knife? A small pistol, perhaps?"

"Nothing," Marko said. "If I wanted to kill you I would do it with my bare hands, and I would have done it a long time ago."

Afterwards, among other sections in his letters to me, Lang would often reflect over how afraid he constantly was of Marko, even though he had no fear of Rauno Meriö, for example, even though Meriö could crush him as if he were a fly. But Lang knew the answer. Even though he was of average height and strong, he had always been afraid of physical violence – never the psychological, social or economic. During the early hours of the morning when he stood in the kitchen fixing drinks and snacks while Marko was in the living room inspecting his collection of books and records, he suddenly remembered a winter afternoon many years ago. It was in the apartment where he had lived with his second wife. Johan, who was then thirteen or fourteen, had a key to the apartment that year and that particular afternoon Lang had come home to find his son and a few friends reclining on the sofa in front of the TV in the dimly-lit living room. Lang remembered how there had been something new, something threatening in the sprawl of the already tall but still gangly bodies and in the barely audible, mumbled greetings that had emerged from the depths of the sofa. Father or not, Lang had felt fear, for he had suddenly sensed the presence of something primitive and testosterone-laden, a newly-awakened sense of territory and desire. And when Lang recalled the teenage Johan and his friends, he at once realized the extent to which he had been self-deluding with regard to Marko. Since Lang had felt intellectually superior to his rival he had insisted the whole time, despite his fear, on treating Marko like a child or half-grown youth who is sowing his wild oats and is therefore wild and difficult but basically immature and not dangerous. But the truth, Lang now understood rather late in the day, was that Marko was an adult, and an intelligent one in fact, experienced and slyly calculating.

"What did you mean when you said I deceive myself?" Lang asked after he had come in carrying a tray with bottles and glasses and ice cubes and crisps and had poured whisky for them both. Marko sat on the sofa and Lang had seated himself in an armchair across from him. Marko leaned forward and grabbed a few ice cubes, letting them drop into the glass with a loud *plop* and then he said, "Everyone is dark on the inside. I probably meant that you are one of those who pretends to be decent even though you're darker on the inside than most." He took a sip of his drink, and when his host didn't reply he went on, "People like you are cowards, Lang. You have to dare to be cruel in order to find out who you actually are. Otherwise you aren't whole, just a half."

Lang wanted to answer Marko the way he had answered Meriö in May; he wanted to say that it was unconscionable to be quick and hard and cruel, that one had to free oneself from cruelty little by little. But he couldn't get the words out and perhaps he remained silent because he was so afraid of Marko's physical unpredictability, of all that was swift, electric and dangerously bottled up in him. In any case, Lang simply shook his head helplessly, while anxiety rose up in him like the returning tide.

"Somewhere inside we're still wild beasts, you see," Marko said, breaking the silence. "When it comes down to it, we do exactly what our distant ancestors did when they faced a sabre-toothed tiger. There's nothing mysterious about a person who kills when he's threatened." Lang looked into Marko's grey eyes and saw that they were no longer cold, but eager and alive. Lang felt a sudden disagreeable connection with the younger man on the sofa, and he immediately sensed why: one sometimes finds like-minded souls, who have the identical answers and opinions as oneself, deadeningly boring, while one can find a paradoxical sense of connection with an opponent who has asked the same *questions* as oneself.

"Can't you leave us alone? Can't you let me and Sarita have a chance?" he asked, staring straight into Marko's eyes.

"No," Marko said. "I can't. I'm your shadow, Lang. You won't escape me."

Lang looked down at the floor and said quietly, "I want you to leave now. Finish your drink and leave."

To his great surprise Marko obeyed: he finished his whisky in one swallow, snatched his sweatshirt, pulled it on and left without saying a word. It was only when Lang heard the front door slam shut and Marko's footsteps fading away in the stairwell that he finally relaxed and started to shake uncontrollably.

Barely a week later Lang and Sarita took a last-minute package trip to Rome. Lang was the one who booked and paid for the holiday. Most probably, he conjectured later, it was a desperate attempt on his part to repress Marko's existence and have Sarita all to himself. But the trip started badly. Lang didn't enjoy flying. He would often say that it was against his nature to submit to sitting strapped in and helpless ten kilometres above the earth in a cigar-shaped tin box filled with thousands of litres of flammable fuel. The feeling he hated most was the sense of being squeezed in like an immovable piece of cargo, subject to inhuman speeds and a horrible display of power he had no part in. Lang always felt an overwhelming urge to run when he sat in an airplane, he didn't want to sit still, he wanted to be a source of power himself.

The flight to Rome was bumpy and as they flew over central Europe in alarming turbulence he tried to explain these feelings to Sarita. But she smiled and shook her head and looked delighted as she gazed down on the Continent from her window seat. Sarita loved to fly.

In Rome Lang and Sarita tried to find their way back to each other. Lang had not told her about his late-night conversation with Marko and he had no intention of doing so. They did everything you were supposed to. They saw St Peter's and visited the Sistine Chapel. They visited the Colosseum and the Pantheon, they sat on the Spanish Steps and drank up the sun and they tossed lire-coins into the Trevi Fountain. They ate four-course dinners in the sunset up on Gianicolo and in the expensive restaurants around the Via del Corso. They spent an afternoon at the flea market in Trastevere and they even visited the Borghese gallery where Sarita pointed out Raphael's portrait of La Fornarina for Lang. Between these things they made love in the hotel room and Lang thought it felt strange and unfamiliar to fondle Sarita's rough and newly-shorn neck. She had cut her hair very short just before this trip.

It became apparent to Lang just how frayed he was. He had developed paranoid tendencies; even here in the eternal city he was forever thinking that he saw a glimpse of Marko. In the crowds at the Spanish Steps, behind a pillar at St Peter's, with a chef's hat in a pizzeria in Trastevere, everywhere this Marko! Therefore it was inevitable that Lang would eventually start to talk, and it happened on the last day, while they were having pasta at a restaurant near the Piazza Navona. He told Sarita about the night of drinking with Marko. Sarita listened attentively, muted, and when Lang had finished she was quiet for a while, but then she said:

"He's searching out your weaknesses. He's playing a game with you and he wants to see who's going to play a better hand."

Lang looked at her with tenderness and asked her the same question he had already asked Marko,

"But why? Why on earth is he doing all this?"

Sarita leaned forward across the table as if she were about to stroke Lang's cheek, but changed her mind at the last moment and leaned back in her chair.

"He hates you," she said sadly. "He hates everything you represent."

"And what is that?" Lang asked. "What is it I represent?"

"It's a bit like with your sister," Sarita said. "Estelle hates you, but she also loves you. Marko hates you, but he also admires you. The way he sees it you have been given all the opportunities one could ask for and you have also taken them, while he sees life running through his fingers."

"The gospel according to Marko," Lang said and tried to sound scornful. "And I take it you are one of the opportunities I have been granted and taken?"

"Yes, absolutely," Sarita said. "And it doesn't help matters that I tell Marko *I* chose *you*, and not the other way around."

"Now back up a second . . ." Lang tried to protest, but Sarita interrupted him and said,

"There's one thing you have to remember, Chrisshan. Marko is smart. He is just as smart as you and everyone who knows him always says he could have been something, if he had just been able to get his act together . . ." She left the sentence unfinished and Lang said:

"I know he's smart, Sarita. I didn't realize it at first, but I know it now."

XXI

Lang and Sarita ended the relationship as soon as they returned from Rome. The question of who was trying to leave whom was irrelevant: they both assured each other that a relationship was not possible under the circumstances and what they thought and felt inside they hardly even knew themselves. Lang gave Sarita back the keys to her apartment and gave Miro a goodbye present – a PlayStation game called "Tony Hawk's Pro-Skater". After that he and Sarita tried to avoid seeing each other although they ended up calling or sending e-mails almost every day, and Lang often told Sarita how much he missed her.

One August afternoon two uniformed police officers, a man and a woman, rang Lang's door bell. The female officer asked if he was Christian Lang, and when Lang said yes, the male officer cleared his throat and asked if Lang knew a man by the name of Marko Tuorla. When Lang wrinkled his brow and gave an unequivocal no as his answer, the male officer gave him Marko's age and general description. He added that there were witnesses who said they had seen Tuorla and Lang together in various bars in Helsinki, also that Tuorla had been spotted getting out of Lang's car in the downtown area one day in March. Lang shook his head in disbelief and said it must have been a mistake, that he had absolutely no recollection of Marko Tuorla nor of any person matching his description. On the other hand, Lang added, smiling with becoming modesty at the female officer, in his line of work he was often approached by strangers who wanted to chat with him when he was out and about on the town. Lang explained that he could hardly be expected to remember all of these people with whom he may have chatted for a minute or two and he admitted that he could not rule out that this – and here Lang pretended to forget the name so the male officer was forced to repeat it – this Tuorla could indeed have been involved in one of these brief encounters with him. The officers nodded understandingly and apologized politely for having been obliged to disturb him. They wished him a good day and the male officer said that he hoped Lang would be granted many more successful instalments of "The Blue Hour" in the future. After Lang replied that the programme unfortunately had been cancelled, but that perhaps it would eventually be revived by another network, one never knew, the female officer pulled out the pad of paper that she had just tucked inside her uniform. She flipped through to an empty page, then with a smile asked Lang if he would be willing to write his autograph with the words "To Elina". The male officer then asked if Lang would write not one but two autographs, the second was for his wife, he said. Lang wrote his name on two different pages and then asked, "What is your wife's name?"

"Oh, you don't have to write that," the male officer said and blushed. "Just your own name. That's enough."

A few days later Lang went off on his annual sailing trip with Uncle Harry. This year, again, Uncle Harry was the one who dominated the conversation. He talked mostly about Estelle. She was much better now, he said, she had probably missed having a home. Lang nodded, but didn't say anything in reply. Harry looked searchingly at him and asked how Johan was doing. Lang said tersely that he was doing well, that he had moved back to London, but that he had a good job and was keeping his distance from his old friends and in this way was managing to stay away from drugs.

They departed from their usual pattern that year, Lang and Uncle Harry, they chose a different route and therefore didn't make it to the lagoon with the dark water and low boulders until the third evening. Then Lang couldn't resist the urge any longer; he called Sarita. Miro answered and said Sarita had gone to the films with Kirsi. Lang was about to ask who was baby-sitting when he heard a man's voice in the background. The voice, which Lang thought sounded like Marko's, ordered Miro to do something and then the call ended. Lang dialled the number again, but the line was busy. Another time – still busy. Thereafter he called Sarita's mobile, but her voice mail came on at once. Lang didn't leave a message.

If Lang had known that his meeting with the two respectful police officers was going to be the last of its kind, he would have, he admitted to me, played it up for all it was worth, absorbing as much as possible of their shy but genuine admiration. In the autumn it was beginning to become clear to him that he was to all intents and purposes unemployed. No TV network had been in touch with him over the summer and he had no literary stipend lined up: he hadn't applied for anything like that for seven years. He read in the newspapers about V.P. Minkkinen's new project: a provocative talk show where the hosts – a twenty-four-year-old man and a nineteen-year-old woman – did their interviews almost naked. Lang realized with painful clarity that he was washed up. For years he had been forced to change his secret numbers every couple of months, but now he had had his number for about a year and no-one called. Day after day his doormat was free of envelopes: no invitations to the TV networks' and the record companies' start-of-the-season festivities, no embassy parties and no VIP cards to newly-opened night clubs or gourmet restaurants. Lang realized he had been living for far too long in a pseudo-world, or rather in two, first the one he had fashioned on his own in his books, and then the intensive, seductive and hermetically-sealed media-world he had created with others. He was no longer friends with V.P. Minkkinen, had ended the relationship with Sarita and even distanced himself from me and his badminton buddy, and he now realized he saw almost no-one who was not a professional associate, or who was simply a friend. On certain days, when his capacity for irony was still functioning, he almost started laughing when he thought about how lonely he was even though he was known to almost everyone in a country populated by more than five million people.

At the start of September he was contacted by a few reporters from the evening papers. They were thinking of writing interviews with questions like "How are you coping with your declining popularity?" and "Entering middle age and falling from the top at the same time – how do you survive?" Lang declined to partake in these. He tried to convince himself that he had never cared about the VIP cards and the glamour, and that he had really very seldom taken advantage of that lifestyle and therefore his fall from the top didn't mean anything to him. But it didn't help. He was forced to admit that the loss hurt even though he didn't care about the industry as such.

Then the blows started to come, and they came in a series of dishonourable mentions that Lang had trouble accepting as purely coincidental. It started with the advice column in the *City*, under the *nom-de-plume* Walter de Camp. As an answer to a question about random sex establishments in Helsinki, de Camp mentioned an S/M cellar close to Åstorget Square and Lang's name appeared as a celebrity who had used the services of the club. In reality Lang often passed the sex establishment when he had parked the car and walked to Sarita's apartment and that, he reasoned, must have been how the rumour started. But the following Friday the gossip column "Flugan" in the weekend edition of the *Helsingin Sanomat* stated that a very drunk Lang had been seen leaving a Sting concert at the newly-built soccer stadium in Tölö. This was blatantly false: Lang was a music snob and had not listened to Sting since the early '80s.

These strange reports continued through September. The most obvious item, however, about Lang's longstanding relationship with Sarita, never appeared. One gossip magazine reported that Lang had behaved in a rude and sexually provocative manner in a perfume store at the Helsinki-Vanda airport, although he had not been there since he and Sarita returned from Rome. Another, a somewhat more serious magazine, speculated about his assumed alcoholism and referred to "sources close to Lang" who were worried about him. The following week another newspaper "disclosed" that Lang and a younger "sportily-dressed" man were frequently seen at one of Helsinki's most popular gay and bisexual bars. That this was also a place that attracted a large number of curious heterosexuals was not mentioned. Lang found a certain twisted logic in this last attack, because he was at this point convinced that the media's sudden, intimate and truth-defying interest in him was due to Marko having put a curse on him.

For more than fifteen years, ever since the publication of his first novel, press radio and TV had helped Lang to promote and polish the image he had chosen for himself. When this same media world now tried to make him dirty and break him he woke as if from a long sleep and finally saw the mechanisms of public life for what they were. He saw how limited and circumscribed such a life was, and he realized that he could no longer try out different identities but had been fixed in a way that froze his very soul, as if he had already reached his ultimate destination and was simply waiting to be thrown onto the rubbish dump of history. He could no longer become anyone else because he was Lang, you know, the guy from TV. When he had written his first novels he had been on the sidelines, someone who moved in the shadows and observed the light where the people were. But now he had been in the spotlight for years and when he squinted and looked around and tried to understand what was happening out there in the ever-changing country of Finland he only saw darkness and indistinct shapes. He surprised himself by feeling jealous of Sarita and Marko and the thrilling freedom that was theirs but which they did not see since they were locked into an ageless game for two, a game with cards like Cruelty and Longing and Submission. In Lang's imagined world Sarita and Marko were free because they were unknown: they belonged to the shadows, the blessed shadows where they could choose freely among many thousands of available identities. Lang, however, tried to meet the interview questions he received as a result of the media gossip with embarrassed laughter and pleading. "I don't want to play any more," he tried to say, but he quickly realized the journalists did not believe him. They assumed he was playing hard to get and wanted to be sought out even more ardently and that he perhaps even wanted to be paid for the interviews. This tragicomic tango only ended when Lang did what he had not had to do for the past year: change his unlisted number and his e-mail address. But while the dance was still on-going he recalled an anecdote that Meriö had told at dinner. In Meriö's story a man by the name of Hamilton wanted to write a biography of the notoriously retiring and for decades practically unseen writer J.D. Salinger. When Salinger, according to his usual custom, refused to cooperate or even acknowledge Hamilton, the latter proceeded to write his book anyway and revenged himself on his subject by portraying him as a kind of PR genius, a hypocrite who, by feigning scorn for fame and money, had managed to attract much more of both than he would have if he had not played hard to get, but had followed all the established rules of public life. However, following the norm would not have done Salinger much good either, because then, according to Hamilton, he would only have been exposed much earlier as the mediocre and greedy profiteer he in reality was. Lang now understood the point Meriö had wanted to make. The person who says he's tired of the profiteering and the hypocrisy comes to look like the biggest profiteer and hypocrite of them all. You either do it willingly or you get raped, it's that simple. And there's no escape.

The more time wore on, the more Lang started to resemble the troubled and lethargic creature he had been two years earlier, shortly before he met Sarita. At the end of September he could no longer stand himself and his depression, and started bombarding her with messages where the wording changed but not the content: he wanted to get together. After ten days Sarita gave in. They agreed to meet for a quick lunch at a well-known restaurant down by the Sandviken docks, but despite this attempt to meet on neutral ground they ended up at Skarpskyttegatan. Sarita half-reclined on the sofa almost exactly in the spot where Marko had sat a few months before. She had her feet on Lang's shoulders while he moved his hips as rhythmically as he could and looked at the little silver ring in her navel. From time to time he looked up and met Sarita's gaze which was clear, calm and somewhat amused. It was an afternoon that contained both the after-glow of a relationship that had once been passionate and the incipient chill of questions like "How did it end this way?" and answers like

"I don't know, maybe it was a mistake from the start." But it wasn't the questions and answers that Lang would remember afterwards, it was the fact that Sarita was so changed and that the sex, despite his own great physical pleasure, had felt deeply meaningless. Because he knew the whole time that she wasn't turned on and that she let him get what he wanted for a totally different reason: out of loneliness, perhaps, or pity, or because she loved him, hated him, or because it was easier to sleep with a person than it was to speak openly and honestly to him; there were many possibilities and Lang could not know which one it was with any certainty.

XXII

Lang's last voluntary appearance in the media was taped a few days after the melancholy afternoon with Sarita. He guested on the entertainment programme "Who Wants To Be a Millionaire?" which was broadcast by Channel Four, a relative newcomer that competed with the Meriö-owned channel that had broadcast "The Blue Hour". Last winter Lang had promised to participate in a special episode of Millionaire where the participants were celebrities, and this was the promise that grudgingly he was now keeping. It should be noted that Lang and the others – politicians, actors, musicians – who were participating in the three different special episodes were not doing this for their own gain: their earnings were donated to charities they chose beforehand.

Lang's guest appearance in the TV studio made him even more aware of the painful fact that he was a TV host without a show, and a novelist without a new novel. He was therefore disagreeable for the entire duration of the taping. In a room behind the studio there was a buffet table with coffee, wine, sandwiches and cakes, and when the harassed host Lasse Lehtinen came out to grab a sandwich Lang started to lecture him in a whiny voice about the humiliation rituals underlying the surface of the seemingly so cheerful TV game shows. Lehtinen looked up from his sandwich, gave Lang a look of surprise and mumbled, "Yes,

yes." Lang went on to say that game shows were not the playful entertainment they set themselves up to be, rather, he said in a pontificating tone, they were a mixture of play and deadly seriousness. The social duty manifested in the initiation rituals such as confirmation in the church, military service and job interviews had now been joined by "participation" that looked like a game, that gave the participants some short-lived notoriety and sometimes even a little money.

Lehtinen shook his head and looked even more confused, as if he were beginning to suspect that the man before him was not Christian Lang at all, not the popular host for the unfortunately discontinued talk show "The Blue Hour", rather a doppelganger who had escaped from a mental institution. Lang became increasingly agitated. In fact, he said breathlessly, the game was cruel, since the often inexperienced guests could control neither their tongues nor their movements in front of the cameras. What was to them the unfamiliar studio environment only made them seem more stupid and ugly than they actually were which in turn, Lang said, made the experienced and confident TV hosts seem more intelligent and attractive than *they* were. To cap it all, Lang was planning to inform Lehtinen, society as a whole was so brainwashed at this point that almost no-one caught the subtle humiliation mechanisms in the format, such as in "Impossible Task", for example, where shy and awkward middle-aged family men and women failed at all kinds of circus tricks, enthusiastically cheered on by their children and the TV hosts who inevitably were young, slender and very beautiful. On the contrary, Lang had been meaning to say, on the contrary the ability to withstand this kind of public humiliation was now taken for granted, so that those who preferred not to participate were diagnosed as "repressed" and were urged to undertake a quick dose of psychotherapy, perhaps with the TV psychiatrist Ben

Furman. But Lang didn't succeed in imparting these conclusions because Lasse Lehtinen had had enough of his volubility. When the polished TV host saw the techno-artist Darude and the model Janina Frostell come in through a door on the other side of the room he gratefully advanced to welcome them.

I saw the programme when it was broadcast. Lasse Lehtinen took his revenge on Lang – with an ironic smile – by presenting him as that contradictory thing, a TV host without a show, as he put it. Despite the cool atmosphere Lang managed well. He raced through the first five or six questions and had already secured a decent sum of money to be divided between UNICEF and the Children's Clinic in Helsinki. Then Lehtinen presented him with the question: "Which is the French phrase for crazy, senseless love? A. *l'amour bleu*, B. *l'amour brut*, C. *l'amour fou* D. *l'amour brulé*." I still remember Lang's expression as he looked into the camera. He had the appearance of an animal being led to slaughter, but the look was also full of paranoia as if he imagined that his rival's tentacles reached into every aspect of his life and that this question was also Marko's doing. But Lang pulled himself together. While a low chord resounded threateningly in the background he looked steadily at Lehtinen and said "C. *l'amour fou*", whereupon a short, dramatic melody announced that that was correct. There was a flash of light and the spotlights made an attractive ice-blue crystal pattern around Lang and Lehtinen, who gave his guest a cool smile. Lang went on to answer several other questions correctly, won an impressive amount of money and received – possibly for the last time in his life – positive attention in the press: Laid-off TV star uses his noddle for kids' welfare.

Late one evening, perhaps one week after the taping of "Who Wants To Be a Millionaire?", Lang was in his office on Villagatan aimlessly surfing one website after another. His mobile rang. He pulled the phone out of the breast pocket of his jacket, answered and immediately understood that something was wrong.

"Could you come over, Chrisshan?" Sarita said without any preliminaries, her voice anxious and taut.

"Why?" Lang asked. He realized that he sounded unfriendly and quickly added, "It's just that it's so late." There was a long pause.

"Are you there?" he asked impatiently.

"Marko is here," Sarita said quietly. "He says he has to talk to you."

"Are you out of your mind?" Lang exclaimed. "If Marko wants something he can talk to me on the phone or come over here."

Sarita didn't answer. Lang's pulse quickened.

"I'm scared," she said reluctantly. Lang thought desperately. "Is Miro there?"

"Yes, he has a fever. He's sleeping in my room and Marko is tucking him in. He was just up getting a drink of water."

"But you're scared?"

"Yes . . . a little," Sarita said. "He's so . . ." She stopped.

"I'd better call the police," Lang said with great self-control and all the gravitas he could muster.

"No!" Sarita whispered urgently. "You can't, please don't! Please!"

"But what do you want me to do?" he asked.

"Come over. Please come over, Chrisshan!" she pleaded. "He's promised to leave if he gets to talk to you first."

"Can't we talk over the phone?"

"I've already suggested that," Sarita said. "But he says he wants to see you face to face. I'm sorry, Chrisshan, I beg you." She sounded more pathetic than he had ever heard her. He paused for a few seconds while his brain was trying to find a way out, with no success.

"Tell Marko I'm coming over," he said, regretting it the very instant he said it.

While Lang drove across town and along the North dock and Sörnäs shore drive to Berghäll his terror deepened. In his imagination Marko grew bigger and bigger and was transformed to an evil idol, an indestructible super-human, a cruel and terrible giant involved in a game he had planned and therefore controlled. Lang wanted to stop the car, get out his phone and call the police, but his fear, after all the false rumours, of being pulled into a real scandal won out. While he drove, he wondered why he and Sarita had not been able to talk honestly with each other in spite of the fact that the impending catastrophe had been foreseeable for so long. When he parked the car on Vasagatan and half-ran along Flemingsgatan he started to experience a succession of images and tastes from his childhood. The flavour of the German hazelnut waffles his grandmother had served with lingonberry cordial. How the evening sun had slanted in through the window of his boyhood bedroom in the suburbs: a thin reddish beam of light that wandered across the wallpaper and disappeared. He saw a young Uncle Harry doing maintenance work on his black Mercedes in a garage on an inner courtyard at Linnankoskigatan, and he heard Lasse Mårtenson sing "Limon Limonero" from the tiny transistor radio that stood on the cold concrete floor in the garage. Lang realized his brain was working in the way that it was said to do in those drowning: he just wondered why the memories that came to him were so flimsy, so banal.

Sarita was waiting for him on the stairs. She let Lang into the building and from what he remembered later they went up in the lift together in silence. When Lang stepped into the apartment all the lights were turned off and it was quiet. Sarita looked anxiously at him and then called out gently "Marko!" No-one answered.

"Miro has probably woken up again, and Marko must have gone in to him," she said, crossing the living room and kitchen and disappearing into the bedroom. Lang removed his shoes and walked over to the window according to his old habit. He saw no outstretched legs, or feet or footstool in the window across the courtyard. Perhaps the person had moved. Lang started to whistle to keep his fear at bay. He sat down at the kitchen table, still whistling, while he waited for Marko and Sarita to come out of the bedroom. Suddenly something tugged his leg so hard he slipped off the chair and hit his chin against the edge of the table. In the same moment he hit the floor and Marko crawled out from his hiding place under the table and threw himself onto him. Soon Lang's neck was caught in a vice-like grip between Marko's muscled upper arm and sinewy forearm.

"I warned you, Lang! I warned you last summer, didn't I?" Marko whispered through clenched teeth.

Lang struggled for air and to free himself and was unable to utter a sound. He heard Sarita run out of the bedroom. She screamed, but not loudly, so she wouldn't wake Miro.

"Marko! Please! Stop, you promised."

Marko ignored her and pressed even harder, and Lang started to black out but could hear the voice full of hate close to his ear.

"You've been at her again, you rich bastard. You've had your dick in her pussy, and I'm going to fucking kill you both!"

Lang tried to call out for help, but he produced only a hoarse croak, and out of the corner of his eye he thought he saw Sarita staring at him and Marko with wide eyes and her hand in front of her mouth. Lang made a fist and aimed a blow at the place behind him where he thought Marko's head must be and felt it strike home. At the same time he managed with an enormous effort to free himself from Marko's grip. He grabbed a table leg and had already hauled himself halfway up when Marko threw himself at him again. This time Lang fell backward and hit his head on the floor and when he tried to get up Marko was on his stomach and had taken a firm grip with two hands around his neck. Lang saw that the undersides of Marko's arms were covered in small white marks that looked like old scars from burns. Then he felt Marko's strong fingers close around his throat and push down and he realized he was about to die, he could not prevent it, Sarita couldn't prevent it, no-one could prevent it. That was when Miro suddenly appeared, he came out of nowhere, his cheeks pink with fever, his blond hair on end and his eyes shiny, as he rushed over to Marko and started pulling on one arm while he sobbed and cried, "Daddy! Daddy! Marko! Marko! Don't! Don't!" When Miro had been saying his name and pulling his arm for about ten seconds, Marko collapsed. Tears began to run down his cheeks even before he let go of Lang's throat and then he got up from the floor, walked into the living room and sat down on the sofa. He buried his head in his hands and blubbered pitifully and in between sobs he snuffled "I hate you all! I hate this fucking world!"

Lang crawled to a kitchen chair and sat on it. Sarita was leaning against the wall by the bedroom, weeping. Whether it was the shock at Marko's behaviour, or shock over her inability to stop it Lang couldn't decide. He was still paralysed himself. Marko still sat on the sofa swearing continually through his tears and Lang didn't take his eyes off his face. Miro wasn't crying any more, he only whimpered a little, and suddenly he walked over and hugged his father and said "Don't cry, Marko." Sarita gave Lang a look of exhaustion and hopelessness as if to say, "He's the one we should feel sorry for, don't you understand that, Chrisshan?" Lang shook his head and said to the man on the sofa:

"You're sick, Marko. Don't you get it? You need help." Then he looked Sarita directly in the eye and asked quietly, "Who is it he really hates?" Sarita didn't answer. She left her place by the bedroom door, walked by about an arm's length from Lang, over to Marko. She sat next to him on the sofa and talked to him in low, pleading tones. Marko said nothing at first. Lang imagined she was asking him to leave, which was confirmed when Marko lifted his head, looked at Lang and snivelled, "Only if he leaves too."

Twenty minutes later Marko left the apartment, after he had spent a long time with Miro in the bedroom, apologized to Sarita, and not even so much as looked once in Lang's direction. Shortly thereafter Lang also got ready to leave and he asked Sarita if she would walk him to the car. Sarita shook her head and said she couldn't leave Miro. She had to stay here and sit with him until he fell asleep, that was the least she could do after all the horror she had put him through. But she said she knew Marko inside and out and she could guarantee he was not lurking around outside. Lang took the lift down and felt sure that Marko was waiting for him somewhere on the ground floor or out on the street. When he walked towards Vasagatan, he looked over his shoulder from time to time and when he opened the car door he checked to make sure Marko was not hiding in the back seat. Before he left the parking space he made sure the doors were locked and waited with terror in his heart for Marko to emerge from one of the long shadows by the buildings, throw himself on the bonnet of the car and bellow, "Stop the car, Lang! STOP THE CAR, YOU RICH BASTARD!" But nothing happened and Lang drove back carefully in the cool, clear night.

XXIII

There is one more incident that needs to be recounted, an incident of an entirely different nature. According to Lang it happened some time in the first few days of November, that is, a few weeks before the night that Lang called me and asked for help, and everything was already too late.

It was in the afternoon and it was already getting dark. Lang had, he said, spent a few hours in the shops and department stores downtown. He had bought some light bulbs, a novel by Siri Hustvedt – it was in a sale, he recalled – an old Van Morrison album and some ready-made chicken chow mein. He was on his way home, half-running since it was raining and he had no umbrella. At Skepparbrinken he encountered an old woman lying on the pavement. She was shapelessly fat, her face swollen and red and covered in small, oozing sores, and she was dressed in threadbare dark blue overalls and an unspeakably filthy trench coat that had once been white. Two plastic bags with empty bottles lay beside her. She was conscious; she was staring up at the lead-grey sky with open eyes while the steady rain ran down her pocked cheeks. Lang wanted to walk past her, just as he had done previously in countless similar situations. And this is what he did. He walked past her with rapid, determined steps, without so much as looking at her. But then something happened. He couldn't. He couldn't leave her there. He paused. He turned and walked back to the woman, stopping a few feet away and asked, "What's the matter? Can't you get up from there?"

He heard how stern and impatient he sounded and he sensed why. Even from this distance he caught the sharp stink of sweat and urine and sick and these smells revolted him. The woman tried to answer, but only produced a guttural grunt that Lang was unable to interpret. He leaned down and put his hands under her armpits and tried carefully to hoist her to her feet. She grunted and swore as he was doing so and a few well-dressed mothers who had just picked up their children from the elementary school on the other side of the street looked inquiringly at him before they pushed their children into the spacious interiors of the waiting cars. When Lang had at last managed to get the woman onto her feet she swayed as if caught in a storm and her legs wouldn't take her weight. He had to support her for several minutes before she stood steadily enough so that he only had to keep one hand on her. With the other he could then lift the plastic bags before he led her the approximately fifty steps to a park bench on the way to Johannes Church. The smell of urine and sick nauseated Lang and he longed to go home and wash his hands with a lot of soap and hot running water. Even so he experienced something during these minutes, he said to me, that was almost like a mystical vision. Because it suddenly hit him that this was what millions and millions of people were doing every day all over the world: they tended, they cared for, they tried to lift those who had fallen. Lang knew of course that some simply did it as part of their job, and others from a mechanical sense of duty. But there were also thousands and thousands of people who did it out of love. And anyway: how important was the motive? Wasn't it the action itself that mattered? The only thing Lang knew as he stood there in the stubbornly falling rain and held the stinking old woman under her arms, was that the protection he had built against reality no longer held up. The walls were crumbling and Lang could no longer repress the fact that despite his evasive manner and his role plays and his tricks he was involved and that he always had been. He, the one who had always warned others about the dangers of not adapting to reality, suddenly saw how perilous it was to adapt to these same realities too readily. He, the one who had always taken comfort in stating that there was no metaphysical evil, now remembered the old saying that indifference was the greatest evil, and he felt at once that he could no longer bear people who masked their weakness and predisposition to hardness, betrayal and cruelty. Lang felt how his capacity for love and generosity stiffly and creakily started to move within him and he placed the plastic bags next to her and without even noticing that he had started to use the formal "you" to address her he said, "Will you be alright now, do you think? Do you have anywhere to sleep? I have to go now, you see. Please try to look out for yourself."

I don't know much about what happened in the two weeks leading up to the fateful night: Lang had been reticent not only about the final dark hours, but about the entire period leading up to it. But with the few bare facts and reluctant explanations he gave me I was able to piece together that he met Sarita twice during those rainy weeks. The transcript of the trial proceedings confirms this. One time they allegedly ate dinner at a discreet corner table at a Tex Mex restaurant in Östra centrum. The other time, most likely Monday, November 13 – they had lunch at a Greek restaurant on Bergmansgatan and they then – although both of them denied this during the trial for some reason – proceeded to spend the afternoon in Lang's bed. From Lang's short, evasive answers to my questions about that afternoon I gathered that he had at that time discovered new, fresh evidence of abuse on Sarita's body. Yet another detail which underscores exactly how precarious the situation was is that Sarita took Miro out of school during the second week of November – "for some time" as she said to the elementary school principal – and sent him to Virpi and Heikki in Tampere.

Regarding the final evening and night Lang was as unforthcoming as he had been voluble and detailed in describing the years leading up to it. This confused me for a long time until I started to sense a possibility and perhaps a reason, which I will come back to. In any case, I am forced to revert to Lang's account of this evening which was concise in the trial proceedings and equally succinct in a later letter to me.

Apparently Sarita called again, this time at half past ten in the evening. She probably said that Marko had threatened to turn up, that he had a key and that she was scared. Why Lang did not contact the police this time and why he had again jumped in the Celica and driven at high speed through the city are questions only he can answer. To me he said that at this point he felt too emotionally anaesthetized to reflect on the danger of again getting into a physical confrontation with Marko. He recalled having some tired but rational thoughts about how he had misjudged his opponent, how he – after their fight in October – had realized that Marko was not an unbeatable superman but in fact a completely ordinary and old-fashioned person with a clearly defined inner core, albeit one that was extensively damaged. Then Lang was struck by the thought that Marko had been as frightened in that moment as he was and at that Lang was filled with the desire to talk and communicate and help. He wanted to make amends for the sinful life he had lived, he wanted to expiate all the wrongs for which he was responsible, to Estelle, to Anni and Johan, to Sarita and Miro, yes even to Marko.

Marko had apparently reached Helsingegatan long before Lang. Why Sarita had not put the chain on the door and refused to let in her extremely unbalanced ex-husband is one of the many questions that received an unsatisfying answer during the police questioning as well as during the trial itself. A matchbook stuck in the front door prevented it from locking and when Lang took the lift up he heard low but heated voices issuing from the apartment. At some point Sarita then – with or against Marko's wishes – let Lang into the apartment and after that everything went very quickly. So quickly, in fact, that the neighbours had no chance to react and call the police until everything was quiet again. A fistfight broke out between Lang and Marko and the latter soon gained the upper hand and once again got a stranglehold on Lang's throat. That was how Lang explained the red marks on his neck when he was arrested. At this stage Sarita begged and pleaded with them to stop fighting before someone got hurt and to her own surprise she managed to break it up. But after a short truce which no doubt was interspersed with heated accusations being flung back and forth across the room, Marko then apparently hurled himself on Sarita and with such violence that Lang said during the trial that he had feared for Sarita's life. And it was then, in his despair, that Lang picked up the heavy cast-iron frying pan on Sarita's stove and took a wild and desperate aim at the back of Marko's head, a blow that was compounded by the fact that Marko hit his head against the kitchen counter as he fell. Thereafter Lang threw himself at the unconscious, possibly already dead, Marko and gave him two more blows, both in the temple on the left side.

Sarita became hysterical and, Lang said, wanted to call the police. According to the trial proceedings she had no memory of the hours after the killing: she was in an acute state of shock and did not come to until the following morning when she willingly gave herself up to the police. Lang tidied up as well as he could and then slipped five large plastic bin bags over Marko's body, three over his legs and two from the top, whereupon he secured them with masking tape around the middle. Then he wrapped the body in Sarita's bedroom rug and squeezed the resulting package into the lift. He said good-bye to the confused and weeping Sarita and tried to convince her that everything was going to be alright. Once he was down on the ground floor he hid the rolled rug in the dark passage out towards the courtyard while he fetched the Celica from where it was at Björn Park. Somewhere along the way – this did not emerge during the trial – he stopped at a phone booth and called me and pleaded for help. Thanks to the rainy, windy night all of Helsingegatan was deserted and dark and Lang therefore managed to force the rolled rug with its grotesque freight into the narrow boot of the sports car, whereupon he drove down to Tölö Square where I was waiting for him.

Lang was apprehended in a section of forest a short distance from a fashionable area in Esbo a few minutes before half past five in the morning. He was caught red-handed: the pit was almost finished and the rolled-up rug with Marko's body was waiting by the edge to be shoved in and covered over. After I had left the Teboil café in Brunakärr, Lang had at first driven around aimlessly, panicky and at a loss, but had then decided to bury Marko in the thick, wild section of forest in the Mankan area. He had lived out there for a few years during his second marriage and therefore knew it well.

The police would not have been able to catch Lang so soon but for a not yet toilet-trained Labrador puppy by the name of Ozmo. Ozmo's owner or, more precisely, the father of three daughters who had pleaded their way to a dog, had taken him out as early as half-past four in the morning and spotted a man dragging a large, bulky item into the forest. The dog owner grew suspicious and called the police. A patrol car drove into the area only fifteen minutes later, but because of the unusual nature of the call the two officers called for back-up. A canine unit arrived at thirteen minutes past five and in this way Lang was arrested by a posse worthy of his status as national celebrity and media-hero: five armed police officers and two trained German Shepherd dogs who, Lang later recalled, growled menacingly at the precise moment the blinding spotlight was turned on and the sharp command was issued. Lang's only observation subsequently was that he did not understand how the police had managed to get so close without his noticing them; it was dark, of course, as dark – he said with a shiver – as inside a bag, except for the thin light from his flashlight, but it was also quiet so he must have been so deaf from panic and apprehension that he heard nothing, no approaching steps, no twigs snapping, nothing until he stood there blinking into the sharp light and heard the military-style commands and realized it was all over.

XXIIII

During the trial, the defence strongly emphasized the individual's right for self-defence, presuming a life-threatening situation, and also made a great deal of Sarita and Lang's state of shock and panic before the death blow was delivered. Lang himself spoke several times during the proceedings and at one of these instances he said, according to the transcript, "Inside we are still wild beasts. We work according to the same principles as our distant ancestors when they were threatened by a sabre-tooth tiger. This is how we are. There is nothing mysterious and nothing immoral about a person who kills under the threat of death."

I couldn't help smiling in secret at all this talk of shock and panic, because Lang had had enough presence of mind to stop and call me from a phone booth rather than pick up his mobile, from which the calls could easily be traced. As for me, as I mentioned at the outset, I was at that time scared witless that I would be dragged into a media circus. But now as I write this I am ready for the possible ramifications, for the mauling my reputation as an upstanding citizen may receive; I doubt, however, that I will be tried for aiding and abetting this long after the fact.

Another piquant detail is that the prosecuting attorney tried to imply that the murder was only the tip of the iceberg. He claimed that Lang must have been deeply involved in Marko's drug deals, not to mention other shady business, and that he killed his partner in crime because of financial disagreements. The prosecutor referred here to the fact that Lang had, among other absurdities, lied bare-faced to two police officers, denying that he knew Marko, in spite of witness accounts of them in the bar and of them talking together in Lang's car. Here Lang defended himself as vigorously and vehemently as he had earlier adamantly shouldered full responsibility for Marko's death: he pointed out that among other things a life in the public eye effectively limited one's means of dealing in drugs and stolen goods without the prospect of immediate apprehension.

The prosecutor also tried, to the best of his ability, to have Sarita charged with being party to the crime. He set out several points that did not match up, among these the fact that she had displayed no trace of wounds, bruises or other marks of Marko's alleged attack, the one that had persuaded Lang to believe her life was in danger and that had supposedly provoked the desperate blows with the cast-iron frying pan. The prosecutor said that all accounts of how Sarita had behaved before, during and after the crime were vague and unsatisfactory: the defence was hiding, he said, in an unacceptable way behind Sarita's supposed state of shock, but which she could hardly have found herself in prior to the crime. In addition, the prosecution wanted to direct the attention of the judge to the fact that Lang and Sarita's accounts were almost too neatly similar, in a way that could be deemed rehearsed. But all of these indications and speculations weighed lightly in relation to the fact that Lang had confessed to the crime on numerous occasions and that he had repeatedly painted a picture of Sarita as brittle and sensitive and someone who for a long time had been paralysed with fear by the escalating conflict between himself and Marko.

Lang's interpretation of Sarita's current state of mind was unwittingly corroborated by Miro, who was gently questioned by the authorities before being allowed to return to Helsinki and to Sarita's custody. The case against Sarita was dismissed. A social worker was appointed to keep an eye on her and on Miro for a year after the trial was over, but there were no other consequences. But I have never for that reason fully believed in Lang's self-assumed guilt. There were several problematic aspects and a screaming lack of logic in his and Sarita's well-matched accounts of how the murder had happened. The prosecutor saw this but had no possibility of making anything more of his suspicions.

For example, I have trouble believing that Marko would have let go of his stranglehold on Lang's throat simply because Sarita asked him to, only to lunge at her afterwards. And my most important objection is that Marko would definitely never have turned his back on Lang, not after their series of fraught interactions with violence barely repressed, definitely not after their fight in this same apartment in October, and definitely not if he had been trying to strangle Lang barely a moment before. It is more plausible that Marko still trusted Sarita and did not anticipate any assault from her direction: even in the act of strangling Lang he may have believed his power over Sarita would make it impossible for her to jump in. Physically Sarita was strong enough to deliver the blows with the cast-iron pan. She was a good bit taller than 170 cm and thanks to Lang I know that she worked out regularly. And her prints were on the pan handle, right along with Lang's.

There is not much else to say about Lang. After his temper tantrum during my last visit to the prison we exchanged a number of letters. His anger over my treatment of his story ebbed away, but in spite of this his letters grew shorter and more remote.

Finally they contained no information whatsoever, at least not anything that could shed new light on his story. In the last letter I received, Lang thanked me in an impersonal way for taking an interest in his case and hoped, without a hint of irony in his choice of words, that my book about him would do well when I eventually published it. In conclusion he doled out some aphoristically sharpened thoughts about the superior indifference in the life that carries on, hectically and restlessly, nonchalantly ignoring famous as well as unknown misfortunes. After that my letters were returned unopened, and in reply to my inquiries the prison director informed me that Lang had instructed his lawyer to return them. According to the director, Lang had retreated altogether from the world, and had all his mail sent first to his lawyer to be sifted according to his instructions. In response to my direct question, the director said that Lang spent his days reading books and learning languages and that the only visitors he had allowed during the past six months were Johan and Estelle, who had each come to see him once.

Sometimes I have taken comfort in the fact that Lang has now had time to cure the ossification of his soul that the hectic pace of his life had brought about. I have imagined that he has used the years of compulsory confinement to find his way back to his living core. Another and at least as plausible a possibility is that he has been psychically broken. He is due to be released in a few months. Then we'll see. And then I will also find out what he thinks of the fact that I ended up publishing this account of his story.

There is one more thing to tell. During the initial phase of working on this book I looked for Sarita with the intention of interviewing her, but she seemed to have vanished without trace. Almost two years after Marko's death, when I had already written a second version, Lang having reacted so violently to the first draft, I published another novel, at best passable near-contemporary narrative which to my surprise became quite popular. It not only sold well but it was nominated for several literary prizes and earned me an invitation to the Independence Day Ball at the president's mansion. On December 6, Gabi and I glided – she in an elegant wine-red sheath and I in a rented dinner jacket – from room to room and stared at all the celebrities and other distinguished people we met. Among the former were V.P. Minkkinen with a new and paper-thin girlfriend, and among the latter a by now almost white-haired but still ponytail-sporting Rauno Meriö. Fairly early on in the evening, when Gabi and I had taken on the crowds and danced cheek-to-cheek in the ballroom and then found our way out to a smaller room where the celebrities, press photographers and the television teams were, I caught sight of a tall, dark-haired woman. She was dressed in a becoming turquoise dress that bared all of her back and she stood arm in arm with a younger man in a well-fitting dinner jacket but who marked his rebellion against bourgeois convention by sporting sunglasses and a bright blue bow-tie instead of the regulation black. Suddenly the woman turned her head in my direction and I recognized the wide but beautiful mouth, the turned-up nose and the slender figure: Sarita. Despite the distance, and although I had only met her once, I was sure that it was her. My heart began to beat faster. I thought about my imprisoned colleague and childhood friend and how he had voluntarily cut himself off from life, and for the first time I pitied Christian Lang. But Sarita smiled at something her companion whispered in her ear and I was blinded by her being and I couldn't help doubting whether this smiling woman was capable of smashing her former lover and the father of her son on the head with a cast-iron frying pan after she had already knocked him unconscious and bleeding. I felt that I would not be able to rest until I had the answer. I told Gabi that I had to go to the toilet and asked her to wait and then started to elbow my way through a mass of actors, singers, politicians and gossip columnists. But when I got to the other side of the room Sarita and her companion weren't there. I assumed they had gone next door to the library to have a glass of punch and followed suit, but they were nowhere to be seen. I kept an eye out for them the rest of the evening, but to no avail.

FINIS